Woeful and Roses

A Collection of Short Stories

by

I0625996

M.K.Aston

Ryecroft Press

For Jen and Isla

Contents

End of the Line

The conductor clipped a hole in the ticket.

'Thang-yoo,' he said cheerfully, handing it back.

The middle-aged passenger whispered a response and returned the ticket to his wallet. His voice was feeble and the conductor instantly categorised him to be a hen-pecked husband. He enjoyed assessing his passengers; it helped pass the time. This poor fellow with his comb-over and weak chin was definitely a doormat, a timid mouse of a man. Probably a desk jockey of some kind.

He was right.

Derek Pendleton had spent the last thirty-three years toiling away in the community services department of his local council offices. He hadn't risen very far up the municipal ladder, not even made supervisor, but that was fine with him. Promotion involved longer hours, extra effort and a willingness to consort with the bureaucrats that ran local government and that, Derek would gladly leave to the others.

That wasn't Derek's style. Derek's style was gentle, quiet.

And that's why this trip to London had filled him with such horror. There was nothing quiet and gentle about London.

London was the opposite.

London was loud and rough.

London was dangerous.

He peered out at the drab concrete blocks that towered over the dreadful suburbs as they slipped past his window and he thought of Marge at home. She'd be sitting by the fire now watching This Morning or Perry Mason. How he wished he were there.

London was a terrible place to visit.

It wasn't like it was back in the old days.

The British Motor Show. Earls Court. 1972.

That was the last time he'd been up.

Marge had been with him that day and they'd gone on to an evening at the theatre.

The Mousetrap.

Wonderful.

A wonderful but exhausting day and the young couple couldn't wait to get back home.

The train clattered across an iron bridge and Derek saw a small park where young children were playing on swings and roundabouts. It looked almost like an oasis, a tiny green patch of joy and innocence in a desert of drabness and filth.

There was a time when Derek and Marge had often spoken of repeating their trip but the months had marched on into years and their desire to do so had waned along with his hairline. The routine of a button-down existence in the shadow of the South Downs had moulded their lives and the prospect of returning to the capital eventually became nil.

And that was fine with them.

However, Derek's GP had insisted.

'I've made you an appointment with a Harley Street specialist. Doctor Winkelman – he's an old friend – he'll be able to tell us more about the tissue scarring on your larynx.'

There had already been talk of surgery, which was bad enough, but Derek was petrified that it would have to take place in central London.

Daily headlines didn't help.

So called 'postcode' wars between gangs.

Society - crumbling.

Violent crime - on the rise.

Terrorist threat - constant.

Derek had begged his GP to book him in locally but had been told Harley Street was the only option.

He'd lost many hours of sleep fretting over this day and dear Marge had begged him not to work himself up. She knew his heart attack six years ago was but a warning and had since then, tried her best to remove as much stress from his life as she could. To that end, she had wanted to accompany him today but he had been adamant that it wasn't worth them both suffering the London rush hour. Not to mention the expense of a train ticket. Good heavens! Was he paying for his journey or investing in the rail company?

'I'm just going to dash there and back. No hanging around, no sightseeing, no nothing. I don't want to spend a minute more than I have to in that God forsaken place.'

'Well, don't go stressing yourself unnecessarily. It won't do for you.'

Derek's hand moved to the coat neatly folded on the seat beside him. He felt the familiar cylindrical shape of his medicine bottle tucked away in a pocket and a warm homely feeling comforted him as he recalled Marge slipping the bottle there as he stood by the mirror in the hallway saying goodbye. The thought lifted one side of his mouth into what passed these days as a smile.

Dear Marge, how she looked after him.

Blasted pills. How he hated being dependant on them. Alas, having suffered from angina since his late forties, Derek knew they were a necessity.

'It's because you stress yourself so,' was Marge's frequent reproach.

'Dear Marge,' thought Derek, 'how I wish I were at home watching TV with you now instead of being about to immerse myself in an ocean of commuters and tourists and thugs.'

The train pulled into Victoria station and Derek straightened his tie and put on his coat.

He took a deep breath to prepare himself.

He knew he wouldn't be able to relax again until he was sitting on the homebound train but he had studied the A-Z map and planned his route. All he had to do was keep his eyes down, remain calm and get to Harley Street as quickly as possible.

He stepped down from the carriage and nervously joined the surge of people all moving in the same direction. Hurrying across the concourse where a hollow voice echoed destinations he had never heard of, Derek already felt his paranoia rising. He had never enjoyed crowds.

So many people.

So many languages.

So many strangers!

He felt terribly vulnerable. He knew he stood out. He knew everyone would be able to sense his fear, everyone would know he was a small man from a small town, an easy target for anyone with a mind to try.

Derek scanned the station for a policeman – just in case. A pair of officers wearing bullet-proof vests were dealing with a filthy drunk who had been troubling a coffee stand and Derek felt his skin crawl. He quickened his pace and bumped straight into a towering, spiky-haired, yob!

'Wachit, Granddad!' spat the yob, through pierced lips painted black.

Derek's heart leapt into his throat and seemed to bang inside his mouth and despite manners requiring that he apologise, he couldn't. The words simply would not come. He hurried on without looking back.

It's better to avoid eye contact. Keep your eyes down.

And keep walking.

But don't run, you idiot, you'll show your fear. Just walk away normally but purposefully, like you're expected somewhere.

Derek hurried down the steps into the underground station, overtaking dawdlers while trying not to make physical contact with them. He took out his wallet and ticket, passed through the barrier and then tried to calm his breathing as the escalator took him further down into the bowels of the city.

On the platform, more people squeezed him on all sides and he felt the suffocation of a lack of oxygen, as if those around him had already consumed it all.

The train came promptly and Derek found himself herded on through the doors and squashed into submission with nothing to hold on to. Strange faces of all shapes and sizes, shoulders and backs and newspapers, all inches from his eyes.

So little space.

So claustrophobic.

So unbearable!

He wondered how people could willingly do this every day.

The train moved off and Derek, reaching for the rail above someone else's head, closed his eyes to the hell that surrounded him.

In his mind, he pictured Marge watching television while the Westminster clock quietly chimed on the mantelpiece.

'Think peace, Derek,' he told to himself, trying the mental exercise his GP had shown him to steady his breathing. 'It's a necessary evil but you'll be home again soon.' Whenever he did this exercise, he always pictured the scene from his kitchen window with its view of the not too distant Downs. It wasn't a spectacular panorama but across the rooftops of his neighbours, the rolling green hills were a joy to behold and he often stood and admired their quiet undulating beauty.

The dreadful journey continued, the train stopping and starting. People squeezed off, people squeezed on and Derek - who found himself pushed into a corner - tried to keep his eyes closed to it all as he stood holding onto a handrail. But every now and then fear forced him to open his eyes to see who was beside him, possibly a mugger, a killer even! Anyone of these people could have a bomb strapped around them having chosen today to prove their extremist point.

Derek's heart began to pound hard. He thought of the scenes of devastation following the attacks on London several years ago.

'Please God, I don't want to die here among all these strangers,' he thought, his eyes taking in the multitude of faces. Suddenly, he made eye contact with an olive-skinned young man and the dark ringed eyes that regarded him back filled him with terror. He immediately dropped his gaze to the floor.

Sweat trickled down his back.

He felt sick.

The fusty smell of unwashed bodies competing with the sharp tang of cologne didn't help.

After an interminable length of time, his station arrived and he forced himself through the heaving mass onto a relatively light and airy platform. Then he was on an escalator rising up out of the tunnelled labyrinth of heat, noise and confusion.

Making his way towards the ticket barriers, Derek suddenly became aware of two young men on his heels and some instinct told him they were trouble. With his nerves at breaking point he stepped off to one side to let them pass.

Seconds ticked slowly by.

He kept a watchful eye on the two of them and waited until they had gone through the barriers and disappeared from view before he took out his wallet and ticket and went through the barrier himself.

He was so rattled and preoccupied with all those around him that he fumbled with his coat pocket and dropped his wallet on the floor. If he'd turned around or glanced over his shoulder he would have seen a dark-haired young man stoop to pick it up.

But he didn't. He was too relieved to be out in the open again and he rushed towards the exit.

Finally, air!

It wasn't fresh air like that of home but it was air nonetheless and despite the crowds at Oxford Circus, his fears subsided just a little.

He was struggling to cross the stream of pedestrians covering the pavement when a whistle from behind caught his attention.

He glanced over his shoulder.

A dark haired man with thick black stubble and a Persian glare was fighting his way through the crowds while pointing directly at him.

Derek felt his stomach lurch.

He knew then he was in trouble.

He knew that this thug, this mugger, this murderer had spotted him on the train, figured him to be a quiet countryman, an easy picking and had targeted him. His only hope was to find a policeman.

Forgetting his manners, Derek pushed his way to the edge of the pavement. He looked around for a policeman but with so many people filling his vision, moving this way and that way, shoving, hurrying, talking into phones, shouting, that he couldn't distinguish one person from another.

He threw a glance over his shoulder and saw the man again. He was mouthing something and his lips were drawn back in a vicious, white snarl.

He looked mad, insane.

Derek's heart pounded, the soundtrack of central London drowned out by the blood pumping in his ears.

He had to get away.

Panic seized him.

The man behind called out.

Derek leaped off the kerb and ran to the central reservation, his senses wild with alarm. His breathing was out of control now but he was too terrified for his mind to picture the view from his kitchen window.

He looked behind him again.

Amidst the crowds on the pavement, his pursuer was holding something high up above his head. Something small and black.

A gun?

A grenade?

Derek couldn't tell. He couldn't make sense of anything now.

The man stepped off the kerb towards him, grinning like a psychopath.

Derek ran.

He heard someone shout followed by the squeal of tyres. Someone else screamed and then suddenly he was knocked violently off his feet.

For several seconds, there was an eerie quiet and the only sound he heard was his heart pounding inside his chest.

Then, he hit the ground hard, landing on his shoulder and banging his head and the eerie quiet erupted into a melee of aural confusion.

Above, the pale grey sky looked down on him without interest as his brain began registering pain.

It came from all over his body but mostly from inside his chest. It felt like someone was standing on him, crushing him. It was agony.

He couldn't breath and he couldn't move.

Derek was petrified.

Then, faces came into his field of vision. Concerned faces. A variety of voices too, different languages all muddling together. He suddenly saw the bearded, shadowy face of his pursuer and the man said something. This, Derek heard as clear as if the two men were alone together.

'I was trying to give his wallet back. He dropped it in the tube station and I was just running after him.'

The pressure on Derek's chest was unbearable and he knew he was in serious trouble. He thought of Marge, sitting by the fire watching TV, the clock chiming gently on the mantelpiece.

'You shouldn't stress yourself so,' she said to him.

The pain became everything, blinding him.

Derek gasped aloud and opened his eyes in terror.

'Sorry to wake you, Sir, but we've arrived,' said the conductor. 'All change. End of the line!'

Portrait of an Angel

'You couldn't have chosen a better day for it,' said the landlady of the Prince Albert Arms. 'It's about time we saw the sun again.' Her voice was clear, soothing and friendly like a counsellor's on a call-in helpline despite being coloured by having lived a rural life. But she wasn't local. She was from further south and possibly west. She was generously built and wore her tinted hair in an unfussy shoulder-length style. Her dress sense was practical rather than glamorous but then it wasn't the fashion of a woman approaching pension age either, which is about where I put her. She slid a lamb hotpot in front of me and I caught a whiff of whatever clean floral fragrance she was wearing. She would've been quite a catch in her younger years. She swiped a cradle of condiments from an adjacent empty table and set them down beside my plate.

I said, 'Oh my! This looks wonderful. Thanks.'

'You're welcome.'

Breakfast had been early that morning and I'd done a lot of walking since then so a calorie-laden heap of pub fare was just what the doctor ordered. To my surprise the landlady remained standing beside me and for a moment, I thought she might be fishing for a tip. But I glanced up at her appealing face with its button mushroom nose and Zinfandel blush and saw that she was looking out the window. I followed her gaze out across the road at the grassy slopes of Y Garn, which swept up towards the cool blue sky and agreed that I'd been very lucky with the weather.

I said, 'I've just come down from the ridge.' I dashed a little salt over my perfectly golden chunky chips. 'The view up there is breathtaking.'

'Rather you than me,' she snorted with a friendly grin. 'It'll have to get a lot warmer before you get me up there. But it is beautiful, isn't it? Anything else I can get for you?'

I thanked her again and said I had everything I needed and with a pleasant thank-you-for-your-custom smile, she left me to it. I unwound a knife and fork from a paper serviette and dug in.

The six miles of Nantlle Ridge had taken me all morning. I walked its entire length, end to end, up and down its seven peaks before lunch. There's no climbing involved. It's mostly a good hike over grass, stone and mud but there's an occasional bit of scrabbling needed on some of the slopes. It's challenging but not technical which is probably what makes it such a popular route. The highest peak was Craig Cwm Silyn at 734 metres and while the views from its summit were amazing, the temperature was not. Down here among the trees and hedges where the sun's rays heated the roads and buildings it was a warm sunny April day but up there, it had been a bitterly cold April day. By the time I had got back down, my core held about as much heat as a carcass hanging in a butcher's walk-in refrigerator. From the car park at the foot of slope to the log fire that now crackled away in the hearth beside me was a mere five minutes but it wasn't until after I'd savoured a pint of local ale in front of the dancing flames and ordered my food that I'd thawed enough to take off my coat.

The pub was situated on the outskirts of a small village in Snowdonia National Park. The way the crow flies, it was a fraction under three miles to Mount Snowdon but by car it was three times that distance. Such can be road layouts in geologically dramatic areas. Inside the pub it was clear from the framed walking guides and panoramic photographs that adorned every inch of flat wall that its primary clientele were not locals. Tourism was an all year round thing here and the Prince Albert Arms appeared to cater well for its visitors. There was ample space inside the main entrance for hikers to hang wet coats and bin walking sticks. It offered a hearty menu with a daily special and had a good selection of beers and wines. It also had a good-sized 'Pay & Display' car park adjacent, the charges of which were refunded to customers spending over £5. Accommodation in the forms of bed and breakfast and full board was available too.

The pub itself was old. It was built of stone and slate, probably from a nearby quarry, and the floor from the entrance to and around the bar was grey stone worn shiny by a million feet. The ceiling was lined with dark oak beams, which were low but not so low as to make the place seem dingy. Basketball players would have found it uncomfortable but most everyone else could stand up without fear of cracking their skulls. The doors and wooden furniture almost matched the dark oak above but not quite. Wine red curtains were held back with dusty ties and a patterned red carpet covered the dining area. These two fabrics gave the décor its only colour. The walls behind the adornments were plain white.

I cleared my plate and surreptitiously belched my approval. I then returned to the bar for another pint. This time, it was the landlord who served me and after a brief exchange of small talk, I handed over the cash and suggested he take a drink for himself, which he did. Instead of doing the usual thing of accepting it for later when perhaps he could enjoy a quiet drink before closing up he came out from behind the bar and sat beside me on a stool.

He was a tall, rangy man of about sixty with a horseshoe of grey hair sitting low on his head just above his ears. He wore thin-rimmed glasses that sat low on his bell-shaped nose and his shirt and trousers were neatly pressed. He seemed well suited to his trade with the characteristic cheery banter of all good pub owners. I found him instantly likeable.

Over the course of the next fifteen minutes, during which he had to get up four times to tend bar, he told me that he and his wife were originally from Bristol. He had spent most of his life on his feet selling insurance and she had been (when not bringing up their two children) assistant manager of a little restaurant in the Castle Park area of the city. However, on their silver wedding anniversary, they had made the decision to shake things up a bit and to follow a dream of finding a nice little pub in their favourite part of the world. He declared with unashamed pride that, 'We may have been in our fifties but we always wanted to be masters of our own little domain. We knew it would be hard work but we were well up to the challenge.' He said the work had got easier after the first few years but now that they were getting on a bit, it was starting to get hard again. They were both approaching retirement age and were now looking for their next move.

'And what's that?' I enquired, draining my glass.

A wistful smile played across his mouth before he replied. 'We love it here, we really do. There's few more beautiful places to live on this earth but we both want a little more warmth and sunshine these days.'

'Ah. So somewhere abroad?' I ventured.

'We don't really know. I like Spain but she can't stand the fact they don't speak English there.' He raised his chin to indicate the landlady as she drifted past carrying an armful of dirty plates towards the kitchen.

'Well, where in Spain did you have in mind? A lot of the coastal regions are full of ex-pats aren't they so the language shouldn't be a issue."

'Very true,' he said getting off his stool. 'I guess I'll have to work on her a little more.' He went to the hearth and placed a ham-sized log on the fire. A shower of sparks rushed up the chimney amid a fresh wave of crackling.

Coming back, he noticed that my glass was empty again and insisted on buying me my third. When he returned to his stool, he directed the conversation onto me.

'So, you're on holiday?'

I replied, 'Not exactly.'

'Well, you look like you are with your walking togs. On your own?'

'Afraid so.'

'Now what's a young fella like you doing up here on your own if it's not for the mountains?'

'Oh, marking an anniversary I suppose. I've been here before but I was a little happier last time. I guess I'm looking for closure.' I suddenly had an overwhelming urge to get drunk and I took a large draught from my fresh pint.

'Say no more. Women eh?'

'Afraid so.'

'This girl, she was here with you before?' His probing wasn't especially welcome but the beer was loosening me up. I nodded.

He asked, 'So what happened?'

I took a breath and sighed. 'She left me.'

'Ah, the path of truth love, eh?' For a stranger, his compassion felt remarkably genuine. Tending bar had obviously given him a sympathetic ear. 'But you shouldn't be wasting your time dwelling on a failed relationship. A good looking guy like you shouldn't find it too hard to find someone else. Listen, sometimes it takes a while to find the right one, you know? It certainly did me. I can't tell you how many girlfriends I had before finding my nearest and dearest.'

His nearest and dearest appeared behind the bar with a damp cloth in her hand and began rinsing it in a sink I couldn't see.

'What are you bending this poor man's ears with?' she asked. Whether she'd heard his boast or not was hard to tell but her smile was mildly sardonic.

'Just telling this young fella how lucky I was when I met you,' he replied with a measured amount of sarcasm.

'Yes, lucky for you,' she quipped. 'But I've been rueing the day ever since.' The wink that accompanied her retort suggested that they were perfectly happy together and I took another long draught of beer to hide my envy. She then asked him if he could finish loading the glass washer and as he set to her request, I wandered over to the fire to warm the backs of my legs. I spent the next fifteen minutes mulling over the landlord's comment about wasting time dwelling on the past and how it can take a while to find the right one. Then I returned to the bar for a fourth pint.

By mid-afternoon the pub had all but emptied of the lunchtime crowd. There were a few lingering diners finishing up or deciding whether they had room for a dessert and a clutch of walkers warming themselves with pots of tea. But otherwise, I was the only person this side of the bar. Through the ale pump handles arranged along the bar like a row of tenpin skittles wearing medals, I could see a couple of obvious locals in the other bar nattering away like hens. One wore a cloth cap like a favoured expression, the other sported a pullover that was two colours too bright.

The landlady and a young helper bustled around the dining area collecting empties and wiping tabletops and removing anything else that didn't belong on a clean table. The landlord came in cradling a few kilos of logs to replenish the basket by the hearth and just for good measure, he positioned another log into the fire.

'So, you were up the ridge this morning, were you?' he asked, brushing his hands together to indicate he was finished.

'Yes I was. Isn't it beautiful up there? You can see for miles. Snowdon looked awesome this morning in the sunshine.'

'If it's really clear, you can see the coast. But it's not always so nice.' He returned to his stool beside me. Then, with a quick glance at my glass he asked in a - you do realise you've had too much drink to drive, don't you? - way, 'Where are you staying?'

'At a little B&B near Talysarn. My car's there too so I'll need to think about heading back in a while.'

'You thinking of walking back? There is a bus you can catch, from right outside here in fact. It runs every hour.'

'Yes, I know. I've been here before remember.'

'Of course.'

'So, do you ever get up there?' I asked, pointing to the lofty green hills that dominated the view out the window.

'I have been up there – once or twice, but we don't really get the time. You've heard about our mysterious angel?'

I told him that I hadn't but that it was always fun to hear of old local legends.

'Oh no, this isn't old. This is a recent story from one of our regulars. At least he was a regular until he died last year.'

'Ok, well go on,' I said, settling myself comfortably on a stool. The landlord was still working on the same pint I'd bought him a while ago and he took a mouthful of it now as if his vocal chords needed fuel for the journey.

'Well,' he began, 'we used to get an old boy in here by the name of Walter Allen. He'd lived here in the village for thirty odd years in one of the cottages next to the shop but originally he came from down Caerphilly way where he used to be a miner, like his old man. But when they closed the mine in the '80s, he packed it in and moved up here to be nearer his kids in Caernarfon. Anyway, like most of those old miners, he liked a drink and was in here almost every night sitting in the armchair by the fire round in the other bar nursing a pint or three. That was his spot. I used to joke that he spent more time here than I did, which I suppose over the years, is probably true.

'Anyway, despite being well into his sixties he was still as fit as a fiddle and he used to walk up Y Garn almost every day.'

'Wow, every day?' An impressive feat, especially for an old man, I thought.

'Well, not if the weather was really bad,' continued the landlord, 'but certainly on days when most of us would've preferred to stay indoors.' He took a quick sip from his drink. 'He said it kept his dusty old ticker ticking. Anyway, he'd usually get up there, have a smoke then come straight back down, which was about an hour and a half's work but occasionally, he'd continue along to his favourite part of the ridge which was Trum y Ddysgl. That's a little further on and involves traversing a narrow ridge that can be pretty tricky.'

I said that I was familiar with it and swigged my beer.

'Then one day, around six months before he died he just stopped going. Stopped altogether. For a few days he didn't even come in here, which was really unusual because like I said, he was in here come rain or shine, in sickness or in health. We all thought he was dying. And he wouldn't tell anyone why either. Of course, we all reckoned he'd had a lucky escape up there with a fall or something, something that shaken the old fella up, you know? There was still a bit of snow and ice up there at the time I remember. Anyway, something had happened and made him realise that perhaps he wasn't as young as he liked to think. And then one night about a week later when he was fairly well oiled, he confided to a few of us round there in the bar what had happened.'

The landlord paused in his narrative for a few seconds - possibly for effect - and took another sip from his glass. It felt like a drum roll was needed.

'Let me just say here that it wasn't like old Walt to make things up, ok.' The landlord's abrupt defensive comment sounded like an interjection from an opposing barrister. I supposed he wanted me to think of old Walt as a sane pragmatic sort of gent and not a crackpot.

'Anyway, he said on that particular day he'd started off around noon, which was a little later than usual because he said his wife had nagged him all the previous day to fix a bathroom tap for his neighbour. But it was a fine day in early April with blue skies and a good forecast. Probably around this time last year actually. We hadn't had much rain at that point and the ground was cold and hard and like I said, there was a touch of snow on the higher ground. He took the direct route from the main car park and was up on the summit of Trum by around two-thirty but just as he was about to turn back, thick clouds came in from the east and produced a whiteout.'

He stopped here and asked me if I knew what a whiteout was and when I said I did, he seemed mildly disappointed. The memory of my one and only experience in a whiteout still had the power to bring on nervous perspiration. I'd been hiking in the Pyrenees a few years ago with my girlfriend Cassie when the cloud rolled in so thickly we couldn't distinguish ground from sky, literally. It was like blindness only white instead of black. Fortunately, the cloud thinned after about fifteen minutes and we were able to make our way down but the idea of being blind up there for hours, with ridges and cornices and tragedy only a few steps away was pretty damned scary.

The landlord's tale had a brief intermission when one of the parties of tea drinkers approached the bar to pay their bill. Images from that scene in the Pyrenees played out in my mind and Cassie's concerned face lingered there. It was ridiculous how much I still loved her.

'Now, where was I,' said the landlord as he resumed his seat. 'Oh yes, so there was old Walt up there with the cloud all around him. He knew the only thing he could do was to sit tight and wait it out. The forecast had been mainly clear after all, so he assumed the clouds wouldn't be around for long. But they were.'

'Oh dear,' I said.

'It gets worse.' It was obvious the landlord had told this story a thousand times. His pacing and delivery was expertly measured and I was hungry for him to continue. He seemed to be in his element too, relishing every sentence as the story unfolded.

He continued. 'I never once saw Walt without his glasses. Thin rimless things with fairly thick lenses, like the sort you imagine an old professor would wear. He used to say without them it was like looking through a greasy window at an out-of-focus watercolour.

'So there he was, hunkered down on the second highest point of the ridge, the minutes slipping by into hours, the whiteout not letting up when somehow, he manages to drop his glasses and lose them. Absolute disaster.'

'Oh my God.' I said.

'Exactly. He always wore them tied around his neck when he was up there, as a precaution, but somehow, they came loose. Now he's really in the soup. Time was getting on, the light was beginning to fade and now, he couldn't see well enough to get down even if the sun was beating down on his head. But he knew he had to make a move soon or he'd be up there all night and that's not a place you'd want to spend a night even in summer. But it's not a place you want to try getting down from if you can't see where you're going either, particularly the part between Trum and Mynydd. I expect you know how precarious that bit is?'

I did. The ground beneath your feet at that point is no more than a couple of metres across and there's nothing either side to stop you taking a quick and fatal route all the way to the bottom.

Thinking logically, I offered, 'So at this point I'm going to guess and say he didn't have a mobile on him.'

'You guess right. Walt couldn't stand them. Hated them. Saw them as totally unnecessary and an invasion of privacy. I think technology-wise, he was probably still trying to get to grips with the TV remote.'

'Didn't anyone miss him? His wife?'

'She wouldn't have missed him until after closing time, because she'd have assumed he came straight here after his walk so no, nobody missed him.

Nobody would miss him until it was too dark to send up a search party.'

'What about Mountain Rescue?' I asked.

'They're not involved unless someone makes an emergency call and at that point, no one knew he was in trouble. But anyway, Walt knew he was in a right old fix. He was six hundred metres up, the temperature was dropping and the light was fading fast so, poor old Walt did the only thing he could. He attempted a descent.'

'Jesus! That must've been terrifying for him,' I said. 'It's no wonder he never went up there again. So how did he get down?'

'I'm coming to that, fella,' said the landlord with a smile. He was clearly having fun. 'Don't rush me. Walt knew the risks but he knew he couldn't stay put either. So, he blindly steps out, one foot in front of the other. But within ten paces, he froze to the spot. He simply didn't know whether he was heading in the right direction or if he was walking straight for the edge of the ridge.

'Anyway, the poor fella said he fell to his knees and started weeping like a child and praying to God to save him. Which really was an indication of his terror because as far as I know, Walt had never been a churchgoer. He prayed that the clouds hurry up and clear so he could at least have a chance of getting down but he admitted to us that he honestly thought he was going to die.

'Anyway, there he was frozen to the spot when he said he heard someone running down the ridge towards him. And seconds later, this woman appeared beside him.'

'You're joking?'

'That's what we all said. At first Walt thought he was seeing a vision because he couldn't believe anyone else would be up there at that time. So this woman told him to take her arm and that they'd go down together. She had a torch with her and told him that the cloud had actually lifted enough that she could just about see the way.'

I whistled a heartfelt phew. 'Lucky Walt,' I said. 'So this is the mysterious "angel" you mentioned yes? Who was she?'

'He didn't have a clue. She told him she was on holiday but that she knew the ridge pretty well as she was up there a lot. Walt said it was impossible to describe the relief he felt.'

'I bet.' I said.

'He said the moment she took his arm in hers he knew that everything would be fine and that she'd lead him down safely. And that's exactly what she did. It took them over three hours mind and it was almost ten o'clock when they got back to the car park but Walt said he'd never been so relieved in his life. And thankful too. He was well aware that the woman had saved his life.'

'My God! That's unbelievable,' I exclaimed. 'Wow, so she's become a bit of a celebrity around here then. Who was she? What was her name?'

'Well, this is where it gets weird. Apparently, she'd been quite chatty all the way down and Walt said it had been a great comfort to hear her voice in the darkness but once she had helped him over the stile into the car park, she stopped talking and vanished. When he turned to thank her for saving him, she was nowhere to be seen. He called her and called her but she didn't answer. She was gone. Walt was really spooked. He hadn't a clue where she could have disappeared to. He said he really struggled to find his way home in the dark without his glasses, tripping over things and walking into walls and such, and it took him almost an hour but once there, he swore never to go up the ridge again. And he never did.'

'But what was her name? Did she say?' I just had to know.

'He said she told him her name was Sandra.'

At the mention of the name, goose bumps broke out over my entire body and a chill ran through me. 'What did she look like, this woman?'

'Well, as you can imagine, the entire episode spooked him for the rest of his life. Not that there was much of it left. He said even though his eyesight was poor, he could tell she was a beauty. But I guess, under those circumstances - saving his life and all - she could've had the face of a troll but he'd still have found her beautiful. Anyway, he couldn't get her face out of his head and he made a couple of sketches of her. You can see her if you like, we put one on the wall by his chair in the other bar.'

The landlord finished the last of his pint and stood up.

'So there you are. What do you think?' he asked. 'Was he saved by an angel or had old Walt lost his marbles?'

'Hard to say, isn't it,' I said, draining the last of my fourth pint. I suddenly felt quite sober.

'One thing though, he was never the same again. Thanks for the drink.'

The landlord took my empty glass and gave my shoulder a friendly pat before disappearing into the kitchen. I walked over to the window and gazed up at

Y Garn and along the Nantlle Ridge. It was bathed in late afternoon sun and the shadows that defined its craggy bluffs and the sweeping contours of its grassy slopes stretched long and dark.

It wasn't as if I needed anything to trigger the memory because it was there everyday of my life running through my mind like a home-movie projected onto a wall. I saw Cassandra frolicking happily up on the ridge three years ago this day. It had been the happiest holiday of my life. But it turned out to be the worst experience ever because our week in Snowdonia was cut short by tragedy. And it could so easily have been avoided. If I weren't playing the fool, if I weren't chasing her, grunting like a demented ogre, she wouldn't have run, she wouldn't have tripped and she wouldn't have fallen. The sight of her body in its pale jeans and bright red coat lying twisted against the green slope far below still haunts me.

It wasn't very big, the sketch inside the cheap wooden frame that was fixed to the wall behind Walt's chair in the other bar. The pencil was heavy and the artist wasn't a natural but he'd caught the likeness enough. It was my Cassie.

Queasy Like Sunday Morning

The old Vauxhall's heater wheezed as though it was suffering from pulmonary emphysema. The air it fed onto the screen wasn't particularly warm and even at full blast, it was barely strong enough to trouble the flame of a candle but it gave me a peephole to see through as I drove slowly down the road. Overnight, Jack Frost had thrown a brittle lace tablecloth over the entire countryside and although it looked cute, it was bloody cold. The soles of my slippers offered next to no insulation against the bare metal of the pedals, pedals that the nerve endings in my frozen feet barely registered were there. I had only been up thirty minutes yet already it was turning out to be one of those days.

This early on a Sunday morning was generally unknown to me but - joy of joys - Grandpa arrived yesterday on one of his surprise visits. Being of the character that he is - severe, colourful, militaristic, eccentric – his visits are the sort that turn a usually docile domestic scene into a John Osborne play. My weekend plans hit the skids quicker than a bobsleigh pusher forgetting to jump on. Without any discussion, I found myself rudely demoted to the inflatable mattress on the sitting room floor with orders that I find time today to play Gin Rummy with the old duffer and to watch John Mills movies. Terrific. With one prolonged ring on the front doorbell yesterday, my cosy lunchtime down the Stag's Head with the lads followed by an afternoon of Premier League soccer on TV became a non-starter.

But before my rescheduled toe-curling delights of entertainment could commence, I found myself having to go out and buy a jar of English mustard for His Lordship. Mother had made the inconceivable faux pas of running out of the stuff since his last visit and Grandpa, being Grandpa had responded by letting off both metaphorical barrels at close range. He'd bellowed at her like a Drill Sergeant having a bad mood swing, about how she should have checked her supply prior to his arrival and how she should always keep an emergency ration of said item in store because one never knows when it'll be needed to bolster moral. For God's sake!

In her defence, she had given a good account of herself but arguing with Grandpa was like urinating into a headwind – you were always going to wish you hadn't started. She'd told him she wasn't aware he was going to arrive so how could she prepare? Anyway, in his mind she should have known better. 'How can you possibly expect me to eat breakfast without mustard? My God, we're not on the continent are we?' Clearly, he'd never heard anything so outrageous in his life.

Dad, who had been frantically searching the nether regions of the fridge and the kitchen cupboards in a desperate attempt to prevent the breakout of war, found a rather old jar of Dijon mustard, its lid fairly welded to the glass jar. He had offered it like the shameful substitute it was and Grandpa had simply given him a thunderous look of contempt. 'You cannot possibly be serious,' he grumbled. 'I haven't kept this body in tiptop shape by eating any old muck, I'll have you know. Or is it your wish to poison me?' All this from a man who'd dodged shells and sniper fire on the beaches of Normandy. It would be comical if it weren't so despairing.

I could see Mother was struggling to contain her temper, fighting to suppress the eruption that was boiling away below the surface like lava beneath a smoking caldera. So when she'd ordered me out into the cold with instructions to not return without a jar of English mustard but to not take too long finding it - breakfast was breakfast after all and not brunch - I didn't think it a good time to protest.

It was plain tough luck for me that being a Sunday the only person out of pyjamas and doing business that early within a five mile radius was old Mr Winters, our engaging but rather senile local newsagent and guess what? - he didn't sell mustard. The nearest supermarket didn't open until 11am, which I assumed was well into the brunch portion of the morning and so I was forced to drive further afield to a place I wasn't sure even opened at all on a Sunday. Lady Luck must have taken pity on me though, because it did and it was already.

It was one of those organic farmhouse type places built entirely of rough sawn pine and held together with good intentions and creosote, a place where the anti-pesticide brigade will happily pay a premium for their locally grown broccoli and homemade jams. I'd only been there once before to impress the buxom Laura Cottington with a la-de-da ice cream last summer and I'd nearly chocked on my rum and raisin at the price but it was worth it. Later that evening in the back seat of the Vauxhall, she'd shown me just how grateful she'd been for the pistachio and rhubarb surprise or whatever it was she'd had.

After a fifteen-minute drive, at the end of which my windscreen still hadn't fully defrosted, I turned off the road into their five-bar gated entrance. Whoever had come up with the shop's name – The Garden of Organic Delights –was surely having a laugh at the customer's expense; either that or they were taking the enterprise way too seriously. There was parking in front for a dozen or so cars and I pulled into a gap beside a German coupé with a rear wing the size of a surfboard. It made my Vauxhall look like a restoration project – a neglected one at that. The pristine paintwork that stretched over its pumped up curves and the complete lack of dirt in the wheel arches told me it had only recently had its umbilical cord severed from the factory in Stuttgart. Someone here had more money than sense, that's for sure. Still, if they fancied a straight swap...

It was warmer inside the glorified garden shed but not by much and my breath hung around my face like cigarette smoke. The scent of pine seemed to add to the chill but the aroma from the tiny coffee bar in the corner by the cash desk did the opposite. It smelt divine. A well-groomed couple sat there flicking idly through their Sunday Times supplements while sipping on mocha lattes the same colour as their sunned faces. I fingered them to be from the steroid injected wheels outside.

Several customers were musing over the fresh produce cart, fingers and thumbs assessing cabbages and peaches like they were valuable antiques; a few others browsed around the shelves laden with assorted tins, jars and packets probably buying nothing in particular but merely spending on a whim. Barrels of loose produce - inside of which sat big chrome scoops waiting to fill the recycled paper bags with everything from hazelnuts and dried peas to wine gums and dog biscuits - were arranged in lines like the freezer section of a supermarket. It was all here and according to the rustic sign over the door, ninety-five percent of it was organic.

I scanned the shelves for the familiar little yellow jar and found it rubbing shoulders with other tabletop must-haves like vinegar and ketchup. The relief I felt was significant. It was like I'd just located a life-saving elixir or more accurately, the antidote for the poison that was Grandpa's volatility.

At the line for the cash desk, I was tempted by the smell of the coffee until the price put me off. No matter how appealing its aroma there's no way it could be worth three quid a pop.

'Looks like you came out in a hurry,' said the middle-aged woman behind the till. She had a clear, untroubled face and a voice that could soothe you to sleep. The subtle roll of her large hazel eyes told me she had noticed my inappropriate footwear.

'Breakfast emergency,' I said, clasping the jar of mustard as though it was all I was worth. I handed her the fiver Dad had given me.

'I hope you're having more than cornflakes then,' she quipped, handing me my change. I laughed with her, told her it was actually porridge and then left.

Half an hour later, I'm sitting at the table opposite Grandpa. He looks immaculate, scrubbed and soaped, unlike the rest of us with our dishevelled hairdos and dark rings beneath our eyes. His Ronald Coleman moustache is testament to his steady hand and good eyesight and his fine grey hair is brushed smooth against his scalp and parted on the side with a laser-like accuracy. Shirt – pressed and starched. Tie – way too tight. Rod down his back – vertical to the nth degree.

The cooked breakfast that Mother lays on the table is just about the best you could ever hope to find. Plump sausages, thick bacon, fresh eggs – the whole nine yards. It's not something Dad and I get very often but when we do, we appreciate it like a stargazer appreciates an appearance from Halley's Comet. And even though I've seen it before, I pause to watch Grandpa. It's gross but at the same time fascinating. He opens the jar of mustard, stirs a heaped spoonful of it into his porridge and then proceeds to transfer the stodgy mixture neatly into his mouth.

A Defeat to Savour (John Banyon's Reward)

It was a perfect afternoon for a game of cricket and the early June sun blazed down from a flawless sky onto the village green at Barton Whimsey. A faint breeze sent a shiver through the neighbouring trees as it whispered sweet nothings to the leaves and airborne seedlings drifted leisurely on towards new beginnings. The men in their cricket whites moved about the freshly mown grass like a single organism, breathing in rhythm with the game. Their shadows were quick smudges beneath their feet. From a distance, it looked like an idyllic setting, a picture postcard of rural harmony. Village life at its most glorious. But up close things weren't as tranquil as they appeared.

Whimsey were playing host to Totten in a village league match and as the last ball of the penultimate over met with a capable bat, a satisfying crack issued around the field as the umpire signalled another four. A trickle of applause went up around the pavilion accompanied by a hearty, 'Good shot!' as the locals, in folding chairs and panama hats, witnessed their score creep higher. The visitors were camped off to the left, close to the shade of the trees near where the cars were parked and while some of them were known to the locals via other circles, business or social, they were generally aloof and kept themselves to themselves. Totten, a town about thirty miles north, were arguably the strongest team in the league but they had a reputation for being the least enjoyable to play against. They took the friendly Sunday afternoon knock much too seriously and, on the rare occasion when they were actually beaten, they were not gracious losers.

'Come on Ed. Last over. Make them suffer!' shouted out a Whimsey batsman who'd already had his day at the crease. Tom Rymer had scored a useful fourteen but was given out lbw by the umpire. Now he was relaxing in a chair with a can of beer awaiting the halftime buffet. A low murmur followed by a brief eruption of laughter came from the direction of the visitors.

'I don't know why we go to so much bother for such an unpleasant lot,' said a female voice from inside the pavilion.

'It's not just for them is it, Mum?' replied a younger voice. 'It's for our lot too.' With Whimsey's innings about to end, some of the local girls had been fussing over preparations for tea for the last twenty minutes or so. Now that the interval was imminent, they brought it out to the waiting trestle tables. Two large pots of tea and several jugs of fruit squash tinkling with ice cubes were put down beside stalagmites of plastic cups and numerous platters of sandwiches, sausage rolls and other homemade bites were carried out and relieved of their foil lids and cling film coverings.

The men in the field rearranged themselves for the change of ends and a round of encouragement for both teams mingled in the warm air.

John Banyon, captain of the Totten side, had the last over. He was a good all-rounder and their best player by some margin. Last year, he had virtually won the return game all on his own with an innings of seventy-five not out and a bowling haul of seven wickets. He'd taken three so far this match and with six balls remaining, no one in their right mind would bet against him taking a couple more. His physical stature usually made him the biggest man on the field but unfortunately, his size was matched - some might even say surpassed - by his ego. He was a dreadful braggart. Popular among his own side but generally loathed by everyone else, his name had become synonymous in the league with the word obnoxious. The self-made owner of a small fortune through shrewd property investment, he was a forty-something who conducted himself more like an adolescent. He often bragged of his income and rained bogus pity down on those less fortunate. He had an attractive new young wife, (his second after the first ran off with another man), a secluded home that backed onto a golf course and a stable of cars that some suspected made up for the size of (or lack of) other things. His teammates and friends had become accustomed to his childish boasts and knew when to switch off but acquaintances and strangers usually took a disliking to the man within minutes.

Ben Radcliffe, Whimsey's number seven, lean and lanky, readied himself at the crease. The umpire made a signal and Banyon ran down to bowl. He was too big a man to be all that quick but his strength allied to the momentum he gathered on his run up made his deliveries worryingly fast. Radcliffe, more comfortable with the ball than the bat, felt something akin to the fear a WWI infantryman would have felt when ordered 'over the top'. The ball was short and accurate. Radcliffe did his best to get out of its way but it caught him on the thumb and he let out a yowl of pain. The ball bounced halfway down the wicket.

'Yeeees, quick!' shouted Edgar Rattigan, who was already a dozen yards and counting from his end of the wicket. Rattigan, broad-shouldered and affable, was Whimsey's captain and at this stage of the game, their only chance of upping their score. It was a risky run and very nearly ended in a run out when Banyon scooped up the ball and aimed it at the stumps but it missed by a foot, which brought a cheer from the pavilion and a gasp of disappointment from the visitors. It was a strategic run though, a necessary one – for it gave Rattigan the strike. Radcliffe, aware of his limitations with the bat, knew he was unlikely to add anything to the total and as he nursed his red-hot thumb at the safe end of the wicket he breathed a hopeful sigh of relief that he wouldn't have to face down another ball from Banyon. Banyon, blustering and frustrated, red-faced and sweating, flared his nostrils at Rattigan like a bull giving his taunting matador the evil eye.

Banyon began his run up again with the sole purpose of knocking Rattigan's head off, of putting him out of action or at the very least, causing him some kind of pain. It was well known that Rattigan had enjoyed a brief romance with Banyon's ex wife a couple of years ago however, it hadn't been the cause of the separation. She had grown resentful of her husband's ways long before and an affair with another man had been the catalyst for her departure. But it was an association that still had the power to stir bitter feelings within Banyon, despite being two years into history. Rattigan's focus though was on the game and his intention was to score as many runs as he could with the next five deliveries. Just for once, he wanted his team to beat Totten. Just once he wanted to triumph over the swaggering, self-praising Banyon. It would be unlikely to shut the man up but it would certainly feel good.

The ball left Banyon's hand. It was an intended yorker, full-length and straight, but Edgar read it well and stepped down to meet it. He sent it sailing over the bowler's head to the boundary at long-off.

Cheers and applause from the pavilion. Boos and foul language from the trees. Four more for the total.

The next delivery was a loose one, too full of frustration to be any good. It left Rattigan's bat and raced to the cover boundary despite a young Totten fielder's half-hearted attempt to stop it. Its velocity was such that he deliberately didn't overstretch himself. The home crowd was clapping. The visiting team offered encouragement to their star player. Rattigan needed one more boundary for a half-century. Banyon paused for a moment to compose himself. Then he turned, ran and bowled a good straight ball of perfect length. It uprooted Rattigan's middle stump.

'Howazeeeeee!'

A great cheer from Totten drowned out the woeful gasp from Whimsey. The umpire's finger went up and Rattigan started walking.

'Ah what a shame, Rattigan. So close to your fifty,' goaded Banyon. 'Damn shame. You were doing quite well too.'

'No shame in being beaten by a good ball,' replied Rattigan, as he touched gloves with Radcliffe on his way off the wicket.

'It wasn't that good. I've been bowling loose to let you chaps get a few runs,' continued Banyon. 'Otherwise where's the fun. Thought it was time to get rid of you though.'

'Yeah, bully for you.'

Rattigan passed the incoming batsman, teenager Gary Brook, on his way to the pavilion and wished him luck. With only three balls left of the innings it was a formality to continue rather than a chance to increase their score. The tail-enders of Whimsey's eleven weren't very good with the bat, particularly when facing the intimidating Banyon.

Brook, the acne-faced son of a local farmer, couldn't keep his eyes open as the ball approached and flailed his bat wildly at the first two deliveries. The third and last ball of the innings took out his off-stump and brought Banyon's tally of wickets to five. His teammates crowded round him, cheering and patting his meaty arms as they all headed towards the pavilion for tea.

The wives and daughters of Barton Whimsey had, as usual, done a sterling job with the refreshments and as usual, the home players - grateful for the contribution - commended them. The assortment of small triangular sandwiches available was particularly impressive with no less than eight different fillings, ranging from the obligatory egg and cress to the people's champion, cheese and pickle. There were plates of Scotch eggs, pork pies and quiche slices all basking in the sunshine as well as cheese and pineapple sticks and small fingers of homemade cake.

The majority of the Totten team wandered with loaded plates over to the trees to be with friends, to sit awhile in the shade and enjoy a smoke or a beer. There was very little conversing between rival players.

'Not a bad total,' said Jeremy Freeman, the Whimsey wicketkeeper, who was holding a paper plate piled high in one hand and pouring his captain a drink of squash with the other. 'You did a good job out there Ed. Sorry I didn't help much.' He'd gone in at number five and been out for duck – one of Banyon's five victims.

'Don't tell me you think a hundred and seventeen's going to be enough?' chimed in Banyon, whose towering figure was stooping below the doorframe of the pavilion on his way out from the toilet. He was still zipping up his fly. 'You're hoping! I predict we'll have this all wrapped up with ten overs to spare.' A few of his teammates who were still lingering close to the food table guffawed in agreement as he joined them.

'We'll soon see,' mumbled Rattigan, with a roll of his eyes. Drinks and grub in hand, he and Freeman moved away to less blustery air.

'Don't worry about it mate,' said Rattigan. 'It happens to all of us. You'll no doubt make up for it behind the stumps, eh?'

'Hope so. God, I'd love to catch that bugger out.'

'And I'd like to catch him a good 'un upside the head.'

'Or better still, a full toss straight in the crotch.' The two men touched cups in agreement.

'So, Ed,' said Ben Radcliffe, joining them on the pavilion's narrow veranda. 'What's the plan? Who's going to open the bowling?'

'Ben. How's the finger?' asked Rattigan.

'Actually it was my thumb. It's ok,' he said, offering it for inspection. The nail was a dark pink colour and the bruised skin around it had a slight sheen that made it resemble a polished lychee. But it seemed to move to its owners command. 'Not broken, I don't think. See.'

'Good. You think you can bowl all right?'

'Yeah, should be able to.'

'Ok, well I thought you might like to start us off with Rory at the other end. We'll see how that goes, maybe three overs each and then I'll take three with Woolly at the other end.'

'Great, I'll go tell Rory and get limbered up.' Radcliffe, a thirty-something estate agent with a low forehead and a receding hairline moved giraffe-like away to find Rory Dinks.

'You think we can win, Ed?' asked Freeman, over the rim of his cup.

'If we can get a good start and not let them dig in, especially that big lump,' mused Rattigan, with no indication as to whom he referred. It wasn't necessary. Banyon was the only person present who could support that description. 'Maybe. A hundred and seventeen's not great though. I was hoping for closer to one-forty today. We'll need to keep things tight. Not give anything away.'

'Sure.'

'They may be the most unfriendly side to play against but beating them would definitely be the most satisfying.'

'You're not wrong there. Want a refill?' asked Freeman, stepping off the veranda.

'Why not.'

'Hey Rattigan!' Banyon's voice boomed annoyingly, like a barn door banging in a gale.

'What now, Banyon?'

'Don't be like that. You're acting like a sore loser already. Don't mind if I do.' The big Totten man held out his cup for Freeman to refill. Freeman did so but reluctantly. 'So, want to make it interesting? Maybe a little wager?'

'What's the point?' replied Rattigan, his patience with the man draining away like sand through an hourglass. 'You've already predicted you're going to win with ten overs to spare. But I'll tell you what. If you can win with ten full overs remaining, I'll give you a tenner. Full overs mind. '

'What? No, no, no. I can't expect my lads to bat that well. One-one-eight in fifteen overs is, what…a…'

'A little under eight an over,' offered Freeman, with barely any hesitation. He was an account by profession and balding by design and seemed content with both.

'That shouldn't be too difficult for you. Especially if you go in first.'

At that moment, a sound even louder than John Banyon's voice grabbed everyone's attention. It prompted dogs to bark and harassed the crows from the trees. It was several sustained blasts from a melodious car horn.

'Hey! There's my little supermodel. Just in time to see the fireworks,' said Banyon, as he strode off to where the cars were parked. Halfway there he turned back and called out, 'Hey Rattigan, what do you think of my latest little purchase?'

'Looks like a peach. Bet she purrs,' replied Rattigan, nudging Freeman in the ribs.

'Yeah,' agreed Freeman. 'Wouldn't mind taking her out for a stretch.'

Tim Woollard approached the table and helped himself to another sandwich. He was a middle-aged plumber with fine silver hair, strong limbs and a beer drinker's waistline that concealed the button of his trousers.

'Would you look at that,' he said, with a whistle of appreciation. His eyes were focussed on the very pretty ice blue Austin Healey that Banyon's wife had just driven onto the green. She parked up at the end of the row of cars but not beneath the trees and the sun glinted off the chrome around its headlights and the windscreen surround. It looked pristine. She let go another peace-shattering blast of the horn as Banyon approached and then stood up and waved a Hollywood smile at everyone in sight but nobody in particular. She looked like Doris Day from a '50s spy caper in her over-sized sunglasses and silk headscarf and even from where they sat by the pavilion, the Barton Whimsey ladies who were craning their necks made snide comments about the amount of make-up she was wearing.

'Cute,' said Woollard. 'Very cute.'

'Think of the maintenance though,' said Rattigan.

'I wasn't talking about the car.'

'Nor was I.'

John Banyon lifted his wife from the car, which was soon surrounded by Tottenites. Interest in the classic British sports car was high and for a few minutes there was a lot of gesticulating and pointing as the big man showed off the latest addition to his garage. The horn let rip several more times much to the enjoyment of the visitors but the displeasure of the locals.

With all of the opposition over by the trees Rattigan took the opportunity for a quick pep talk. He insisted that their score was good enough to win but only if they played well and kept things tidy. Rory Dinks pointed out that it was twenty-one runs more than they had got last time they played Totten, but then someone else added that they had lost that game with several overs still remaining.

'Never mind that,' said their captain. 'Today could be our day. Now, we're all fit and we all want this so let's do it.'

A volley of 'Yeah!'s accompanied the end of Rattigan's speech. The men binned their plates and cups and while some nipped into the pavilion to queue for the one toilet, most headed out onto the pitch, reinvigorated.

When Banyon and his team realised that teatime was over, they made their way back to the pavilion. Banyon's wife came with them. They pooled a few empty chairs and sat in a group close to the scoreboard. Banyon padded up but wasn't an opening bat. Two other Totten men were already walking out to the wicket.

'So you didn't want to take me up on my wager then?' said Rattigan from the field.

'What wager's that, Babe?' asked Banyon's wife, looking at her husband over the rim of her dark glasses.

'Yeah, what was that again, Rattigan?'

'A tenner says you won't win with ten full overs remaining. That's what you predict isn't it?'

'Ok. Deal. If you want to give away your hard-earned money, fair enough. We'll beat your total in fifteen overs or less.' He stood up and bellowed out to his opening batsmen. 'Let 'em have both barrels, lads!'

The afternoon became warmer as the sun continued inching across the sky. The breeze strengthened slightly and sent a few paper plates wheeling across the grass and the whistle of sweet nothings through the leaves on the trees became an unbroken rustle.

Totten's innings began in moderate tempo and as Ben Radcliffe began his second over, the score on the board was only just into two figures.

'Both barrels I said. Come on!' shouted Banyon from the chair he was nearly crushing.

Rory Dinks, agile and intelligent, broke through in his second over with an appeal for lbw, which was upheld by the umpire.

'Jesus! If you want something done, do it yourself John,' said Banyon, taking up his gloves and marching pompously out to the middle. The pads he had on looked little more than large shin guards on his long legs and the bat resembled a child's toy in his large hands.

'Come on lads,' called out Rattigan, from his position at mid-off. 'Don't let him get comfortable.'

It was an optimistic appeal to encourage his men to maintain the pressure but John Banyon was undeterred. He was in fine form from the get go and as his bat flashed left and right and sent the home-side fielders running hither and thither the score on the board increased briskly. By the time Rattigan and

Woollard had each completed three overs, the visitors were eighty-four for three. The Totten spectators were revelling in their man's epic display of batting heroism and the umpire's arms were swinging up and down and from side to side almost as often as they would have been were he leading an aircraft into a parking bay.

Rattigan needed another breakthrough. At the current rate, it was highly likely he'd have to give Banyon ten pounds and it was a wager he'd made sincerely thinking that Banyon hadn't a chance of winning. But his nemesis was on strike too often and hitting too many boundaries and so Rattigan decided to try a different approach. He brought his fielders in tighter and told his bowlers to keep their deliveries pitched full and as accurate as possible.

'Mix up the pace a little too if you can. Let's see what that does,' he confided. It worked. Batsman number four misread a slower ball from Radcliffe and lost his bails and the next guy was out first ball, caught behind by Jeremy Freeman. Two wickets in two balls. Whimsey's cheering suddenly gained volume. Suddenly the unlikely seemed possible. If they could just keep John Banyon at the non-striker's end, they stood a chance. But it was only a chance.

Banyon saw his bet slipping away. Thirty-two runs in two overs was a tall order, even for him and his teammates were letting him down. They couldn't even get a single so that he could take charge. His leadership encouragements were becoming more sarcastic with each passing ball to the point that his fellow batsman didn't know whether he wanted him to try and hit the ball and get a single or to stay put until the end of the over. When batsman number six came out, there were three balls left of the over and Banyon told him to remain at his end.

'Don't try and get any runs, but don't get out. It'll give me the strike at the change of ends.'

A simple plan but it didn't work. On the last ball of the over, number six, was bowled a tempting delivery by Radcliffe - as suggested by Rattigan - and he played it quite well, passing the fielder at mid-wicket. There was an easy one out of it and possibly a two and he looked to his captain for confirmation. Banyon held up his hand saying 'No, stay put!' but the young lad was so keen to put a number next to his name on the score card that he decided two runs were his for the taking. He began running down the wicket shouting, 'Yes, yes!' and Banyon stayed put at the other end shouting, 'No, go back, you idiot!' Shouts from the visiting spectators beneath the trees and the rest of the team around the pavilion seemed to add to the confusion as the two batsmen did a mad stuttering dance between the creases. The ball was thrown in to Freeman and the bails were knocked off the stumps. The umpire extended his arm and his finger pointed skywards.

RUN OUT!

It was a point of contention for a few minutes because Whimsey obviously wanted it to be Banyon who was out as he had clearly refused to run however the umpire suggested that the rules stated it was the batsman nearest the put down wicket that was out. And in this case that batsman was number six. So number six slouched back to the pavilion with his head hung low, a zero next to his name on the scorecard and a curse under his breath.

Banyon was infuriated with his team's poor performance however, he was glad to be at the striker's end again. With thirty-two runs needed, it would need a miracle of no balls and overthrows for him to not lose his bet but unless his teammates could survive the remaining eleven overs, Totten would lose the match as well.

'What's up Banyon?' Rattigan teased. 'Not going your way? Looks like you owe me a tenner.'

'Don't count your chickens, Rattigan,' he bellowed back, as he surveyed the defensive field. 'I can do a lot of damage with six balls.' The number seven batsman came to the crease with a worried expression on his young face.

'Ok, lads. Let's keep it tight. Come on!' shouted Rattigan, as he turned at the end of his run up. His first delivery was hit for four. His second could have added one or two more but Banyon decided to stay put. His strategy was to get a single on the last ball of the over and only boundaries the rest of the time. Rattigan's third delivery went to the keeper, as did the fourth. The fifth was hit for six much to the delight of the Totten supporters but the last ball found the keeper's gloves again.

'That's a tenner, thank you very much,' gloated Rattigan, as he passed by Banyon on his way to congratulate his wicketkeeper.

'You're still going to lose the game, Rattigan.' Banyon's face glowed with humiliation and loathing.

'I already feel like a winner, thanks.'

'It's about all you will win, today. Twenty-two runs in ten overs is something even you could do.'

'What a tool,' said Freeman, as Rattigan patted his wicketkeeper on the shoulder.

'Isn't he? Keep up the good work though Jem. We're not beaten yet. They've got four men left and we've got every chance of bowling them out but we must keep Banyon down that end of the wicket.'

Rattigan gave the ball to Woollard and breathed instructions into his ear.

All the time Banyon was off strike, they had a chance. Number seven had a lot of pressure on him – pressure that increased significantly when Rattigan brought in two fielders for the close catch.

'Whatever you do, don't get out,' said Banyon from down the wicket. 'You don't even need to score. Just defend your stumps, ok?' Number seven nodded. He didn't look confident.

Woollard bowled. It was pitched up and the Totten batsman dropped to his knees to get out of its way. Freeman caught it comfortably behind. Number seven's knees wobbled a little. The next ball, a slower one, went harmlessly past his off stump. The third would have hit off stump had he not stepped forward and defended. The fourth ball was pitched up again and found ten feet of air off his bat handle.

'Howzzeeeee!' called several voices in unison as the rest of the field held their collective breath. The fielder at silly mid-off moved under the ball and caught it with both hands and a great cheer went up around the green. Number seven looked helplessly at Banyon and walked off the wicket as the umpire's finger went up. Banyon shook his head. He was running out of partners. Woollard was congratulated by his team and told to keep it up.

'You're on fire today, Woolly,' said Will Werner, the middle-aged painter and decorator who'd caught the ball.

The next two balls of the over did nothing to concern the visitor's eighth batsman. But as Rattigan ran down to bowl to Banyon once again after the change of ends, the odds swung back in Totten's favour. Rattigan bowled a good straight over but Banyon, believing that it was now or never as far as him being able to score the winning runs, played like a man possessed. Two sixes came off the first two deliveries, a four of the third and nothing on the fourth. Six runs would win Totten the match. Six little runs. One shot would do it. One majestic six.

Banyon could taste the win.

Rattigan could sense defeat.

The fifth delivery brought a gasp from everyone present as Banyon swung but missed. But the ball had nicked the inside edge of his bat and those close enough to have heard it prayed that the keeper would catch it. Banyon span around just in time to see it bounce on the ground before it reached Freeman's gloves.

Banyon's relief was immense.

Rattigan's disappointment was just as immense. 'How lucky can you get?' he sighed.

'You're not going to win Rattigan,' stated Banyon, with a matter-of-fact obstinacy.

Rattigan took a moment to reposition a couple of his men in the field. Whether Banyon would try to finish it now or play for a single and give himself another over to do so was anyone's guess but Rattigan and those of his team he spoke to suggested it unlikely they could avoid defeat. Banyon was just too good at scoring runs.

As Rattigan ran down to the crease, he felt as though he was delivering the last ball of the match.

Either way, with eight overs remaining and three wickets in hand, any sensible betting man would put their money on Totten. But it had been a much closer fought game than last year and at the very least, he had won a tenner off his arrogant rival.

The ball left his hand and flew down the wicket. It was a shorter delivery than he had intended. It swung a little to the leg side. Banyon kept his eye on it and moved his weight onto his back foot. He swivelled at the hips and connected beautifully. The ball went sailing up and over towards his loudly cheering supporters under the trees. Up it went. Over it went. A mighty hit. A six for sure.

It arced through the warm summer air with grace and power and all eyes followed its progress as though it were a once-in-a-lifetime comet heralding the end of some great epoch. Passing its zenith, it began to curve down, down, down until it came down on the bonnet of the Austin Healey. The dense thud of the impact reshaping the smooth metal was followed immediately by the sound of splintering glass as the ball's journey ended at the windscreen. A collective 'Ooh!' brought everyone's voices together like a choir cringing. Then there was silence. No voices, no dogs barking, no crows cawing.

'Oh, my car!' wailed a horrified Mrs Banyon, tipping back her chair as she jumped to her feet. 'What have you done?' She rushed across to her car as quickly as her strappy sandals would allow and drew in her breath at the sight of the damage. 'Oh!' Then she threw daggers at her husband and yelled, 'You impotent fool. Look what you've done!'

Banyon at the crease, cursed loudly with one small, strong word. The umpire raised his hands to the sky and the game was over. Totten had triumphed again.

Déjà Clue

Today's early morning weather forecast predicted snow and looking up, I'd say it seems to be right on the button. There's a mass of heavy white cloud hanging low and it looks pregnant with the stuff. In fact, as I stamp my feet to help the circulation and to ward off the cold the first flurries brush my face. It's a bitterly cold Thursday morning. I'm tired through lack of sleep and waiting at the bus stop by the village stores I'm wondering if I'm doing the right thing. It's a decision I've been wrestling with for months now and it's driving me bloody crazy. Over and over the same damn questions and over and over the same unconvincing answers –

Is this really something I want to try? Well, nothing else seems to work, so yes, it's worth a try.

Isn't it a load of old bull? I don't know but it sounds like it works for other people so surely, it's worth a try.

Can I afford to throw money away on something that might not work? It's not like you're spending a fortune. It's a hundred quid for God's sake and it could make all the difference!

These are just three of the questions that have had me staring at the bedroom ceiling for hours contemplating my future. A future on my own. Well, today is going to be different; today I am determined to go for it. Today I am taking a step that could change my life forever. And it's not just because my bed has seemed far too big now for two months and four days. That's how long it's been since Suzanne decided we needed to take a break. "Things just aren't working out," she said. "I'm not sure I love you anymore," she said. "I need time to think about us," she said. If this were a movie script, I think we'd all know the meaning behind that trio of phrases. In hindsight, I guess her decision shouldn't have surprised me, the spark had long since disappeared from our relationship and we spent far too much time arguing over silly things. Or rather, she argued, I just nodded my head and said, "Yes dear, no dear, three bags full dear." Yet I honestly hadn't realised we'd reached such a low. But never mind, one thing I do know is I can't stand sleeping by myself, to reach out and not feel Suzanne's warmth beside me. Since she went back to her parents, it's not just the bed that feels empty.

I'm ashamed to admit how long it has taken me to get to this point of actually doing something but finally last week I found the courage to book an appointment with a hypnotherapist. You see, I have lived with an inferiority complex for most, if not all of my life and at thirty-one years old, I just can't take it anymore. Something's got to change. I'm fed up to the back teeth of being too afraid or just plain unable to assert myself. I'm not talking about wanting to become confrontational; I'm talking about standing up for my thoughts, my ideas and my beliefs. I honestly can't remember an instance where I've stood up to criticism or dissent, whether at work, at home or down the pub with my mates. My conviction is about as sturdy as a sorbet in a sun lounge and because of this, I blame myself for my own unhappiness and my failed relationship. I know Suzanne certainly does.

Well, not anymore. I've reached a precipice and it's forced me to choose between acceptance and action – either shut up about how miserable life is or do something about it. And the truth is, I want to be happy, really I do and preferably with Suzanne, so I'm going to do something about it.

This all came about by chance really. Working in the post room of the local council offices in Amberton, I get to hear plenty of gossip as I walk the floors from desk to desk delivering the daily mail. Most of it is pointless drivel about who's doing whom or what happened or will happen at the weekend party but a few months ago, I overheard something that got me thinking. One of the accounts assistants was praising the merits of a course of hypnosis he'd taken and he went on to admit how in just a few short weeks it had turned his life around. I wasn't able to stick around for the entire conversation - I didn't want to appear to eavesdrop for a start - and so I didn't hear why he had decided on this course of action in the first place but apparently the therapy had given him a whole new dynamic and a greater level of happiness in all areas of his life. Other than by name, I don't actually know this person but a colleague who does, informed me that the man had gone to the therapist because he wanted to improve his confidence. According to my colleague this man definitely seemed a happier person than he remembered, "More comfortable in his skin," were the actual words he used.

Improve his confidence? Bingo! I immediately reasoned that if it could that for him, then it could do it for me and so several nail biting weeks later (seven to be exact! I know, what's wrong with me?) I booked an appointment of my own. No, I'm not going to allow myself to chicken out today. All I have to lose is a hundred pounds, which I consider a small price to pay for taking such a positive step. But listen to me - here I am, already assuming that it'll be a waste of time and money. Christ, where's the positivity!

Inside my coat pocket, my cold fingers fiddle nervously with the corners of my bus pass. It reminds me of the unpleasant man that short-changed me when I bought it last weekend in Amberton. The pass cost a fiver and I'm sure I paid with a twenty but stupid me, I didn't realise until I'd stepped outside that he'd only given me a fiver back. Of course, when I went back in question him, he swore blind I'd only given him a tenner. Obviously not wanting to make a scene in front of his other customers I apologised and left it at that. But I was damn sure I'd given him a twenty. I should have asked to see the notes in the till or at least to speak to the manager or the owner. Little things like that happen to me all the time and it really pisses me off.

During my initial phone call to the therapist – and I was bloody nervous at the time – he explained that even after the first session, which would consist of a short consultation to understand the root of my problem (most likely insecurity, he said) followed by the therapy, I would feel a difference. He told me that it wouldn't take long to reprogram my subconscious mind, to replace the negative thoughts with positive ones. However, he warned that it would most likely take more than one session to change the habits of thirty-one years. But he assured me that I had already taken the first and most important step to a new and improved me simply by calling him.

At last, the bus comes. It's a welcome relief to get aboard and feel the warmth from its heaters. It's about a forty-minute journey to the therapist and I'm dying to get off my feet, which are like block of ice. Being the time of morning that it is, the bus has a few school kids on it, the stragglers who don't want to get into their classrooms too soon. The rest of the seats are occupied with mothers carrying infants or old dears and their husbands off to the supermarket for the weekly groceries or to the Post Office to collect their pensions. The only free seat I can see happens to be beside a young mum with a half dressed baby in her lap and an exasperated huff in her manner. But the seat has a bag of baby stuff in it and the woman is rummaging around in it juggling tiny boots and tiny gloves, trying to find matching pairs, it looks like, while holding a bottle of milk to the baby's mouth. My polite request to sit down in the spare seat beside her is met with a furious glare and a frosty, "Can't you see I'm busy!" Not wanting to argue I accept the fact that I'm going to be standing for a while longer. At least until the kids get off in Amberton. God, I hate it when people are disrespectful. Why couldn't the woman have just been civil? And, as usual, instead of standing my ground and insisting that the seat is for sitting on not putting bags of crap on, I accept the situation and succumb to another daily tribulation. Please God, let this hypnosis thing help me!

I hold on to the overhead rail to steady myself as the bus rounds the corner at the end of the village and heads out into the countryside. A dusting of white begins to settle on the trees and verges.

To my surprise, there are three therapists in Amberton (hypnotherapy must be a thriving business), but I had deliberately chosen one in Felbourne, which is a little further away from my home and my place of work. It's also a town I rarely go to. There is good reason for this. I chose to go to Felbourne on the basis that I would be less likely to bump into the therapist in Amberton or God forbid, down the local pub with my mates on a Friday night. This I deemed crucial if was going to keep this little outing to myself. It was one thing for me to admit to myself that I'm a loser but to admit it to anyone else, particularly Suzanne, was something that I simply could not do. The shame would be too great and I would never be able to live it down. And I'm convinced she would never want to get back together with a self-confessed failure.

For the umpteenth time I go over the phone call I made to book this session. The therapist had explained that our meeting would remain confidential and this had, to an extent, put my mind at rest.

Another thing I considered, and am grateful to the therapist for, is his willingness to accept cash. In fact he actually informed me that this method of payment wasn't unusual and that he was quite happy to be paid that way. If Suzanne does come back and we pick up where we left off, I don't want to have to explain an unusual entry or two in my monthly statement, should she happen across it. I've been so paranoid about this visit and have tried to think of every little thing that could go wrong it's no wonder I haven't been sleeping.

The bus stops several times on the way into town and a few more people get on. Like me, they all have to stand except one particular man who looks down at the free seat beside the flustered mother with the baby and says something assertive enough that she moves the bag to the floor and allows him to sit down. I can't help but roll my eyes in a "Why couldn't I have done that?" sort of way. When the bus reaches the school, seats become free as the kids disappear inside the gates. I quickly grab one and try to relax. We then carry on into Amberton's town centre and within a few minutes almost all the seats are empty as everyone gets off. A few others get aboard to continue on towards Felbourne. Felbourne is smaller than Amberton and has nothing extra going for it so it's a place I rarely get to and as I gaze out at the lesser-known roads we clatter down, my concerns about keeping this mission covert subside because, as far as I can recall, I've only been here a handful of times before in my entire life. Which is perfect because it's less likely that I'll see anyone I know. And hopefully, fingers crossed, nobody I know will see me.

Because of course, I've had to take today off work. I'm attending an Aunt's funeral as far as they're concerned. Although, if I'm seen, well, I'll cross that bridge of little white lies if and when I get to it. I don't know why I didn't just tell the truth…really I don't because I know I've opened myself up to all kinds of grief if anyone finds out. It's highly unlikely but there's always the chance that Suzanne could phone work to speak to me and if she does, I'm busted. She'll know for sure that I'd told a lie about going to a funeral and she'll want to know why. If there was one thing about her I wish I could change, it's that she'd be more understanding. I'm really not comfortable going behind her back or anyone else's for that matter but the embarrassment I'm feeling just doing this is so great, I simply don't know what else to do.

The bus passes a large DIY store and a flicker of recognition comes to me. I tell myself that it must be déjà vu and for a few moments I consider just how peculiar and deep a subject déjà vu is. Didn't I once read a theory of some professor's arguing that it could be related to reincarnation or some such weirdness? I'm not sure if I'm into that. Anyway, maybe I have travelled along this road a few times before. It is possible. Or perhaps the store reminds me of somewhere else – like the retail park not far from my parents' house for instance - yes, of course, that's it – there's a huge DIY store there as well.

Twenty minutes later, I get off at the stop I had pre-calculated to be the closest to the therapist's address. Snow continues falling gently, tiny powdery flakes that dissolve on my warm hands the instant they make contact. I check my watch. My usual custom is to arrive early for appointments - I'd rather wait around for a while than risk being late due to bad traffic or some other hindrance - but today I didn't do that because I knew it would give the coward in me time to reconsider. Thankfully, my timing is pretty much perfect.

It's only a short walk to my destination now and I tighten my scarf around my neck and thrust my hands deep into my jacket pockets. This is my point of no return; the final five-minute walk to mull it over one last time and convince myself that the whole thing is a bad idea. But NOT today! Today is the first day of the rest of my life and I march forward with determination.

A homely coffee shop is close by the bus stop and as I pass, a girl wearing an apron with the shop's logo emblazoned across her torso emerges from inside. She's carrying a damp cloth and a stick of chalk to amend the blackboard that hangs beside the door listing the day's specials. She smiles and says; "Hello" and I see in her eyes the playful spark of attraction. She has a gorgeous smile, a smile that not only reveals a set of perfectly formed white teeth but also radiates from her beautiful blue eyes like warm sunshine. I want to reply with something witty and urbane but instead continue walking past with barely a nod of my head and the briefest of smiles. I curse my timidity and tell myself that I absolutely must stop in there on my way back if only to see that amazing smile again.

I turn a corner and walk steadily down a quiet residential street. My footsteps dissolve the white powdery snow to leave black prints behind me. I take out the scrap of paper I had scribbled the therapist's address on and count the house numbers as I walk - 18, 20, 22 - just a few more now and then 38. Here we are then - 38. My heart is thumping wildly despite the fact that I'm somewhat disappointed. It's not what I had imagined at all. This doesn't look anything like a therapist's practice or clinic (whatever they look like); it's just a regular semi-detached house with a gate in a hedge and a short path up to a front door next to a bay window.

Despite being close to freezing, my hands are clammy and my throat is dry. Suddenly, I want to run back to the bus stop, I really do. I'm standing on the pavement outside the house, hidden from the bay window by the tall hedge and it occurs to me that if anyone was watching for my arrival, they probably wouldn't have seen me so I could easily get away and then telephone to apologise for not turning up. I turn and look back up the road I have just walked so resolutely down. Shall I? Shall I go back? I hover for a few seconds, torn, wondering the best thing to do. Flee or face up to it? Save my money and avert the shame or try something that could make a difference?

NO! The best thing is to do it! So do it! Do it NOW!

I try to swallow the sick feeling in my throat but my mouth is too dry. My legs are quivering but I force myself through the little metal gate, its hinges emitting a shrill squeak as it lets me in. I wince at the loudness of it. I ring the doorbell and the soft, almost dreary ding-dong brings a strange comfort to me and then all of a sudden my anxiety evaporates and I'm excited. All of a sudden, I just want to get on with it. I want the next two hours to fly by so that I can emerge from this door a different person - A NEW ME!

The door opens and a well-groomed man of fifty-something greets me with a friendly smile and a firm handshake. He introduces himself as the therapist and the man I spoke to on the phone. He has a warm, cultured voice and a very neat goatee and he instantly puts me at ease. He invites me in, closes the door and offers to take my coat. I hand it over and he hangs it on a hook beside the door. The hallway smells of laundry mingled with a roasting joint (beef, I think) and I get a pang of hunger. He bids me to follow him along the green-carpeted hallway and into a light airy room off to the right. He waves me in and then follows. Fixed to one of the walls are several certificates headed with important looking crests and hanging across another, a panoramic mountain landscape that seems vaguely familiar. Through the window I see a neat little garden gradually turning white. The therapist signals for me to sit in the comfortable black recliner and I do. He closes the door with a muted click and I hear him take a deep, measured breath.

This man is a charlatan. He knows my situation, my weaknesses and the difficulties I am having. He's known it for some time now. For the next ninety minutes, he'll keep me in a quiet state of deep relaxation and hypnotise me into thinking that I have never been here before and that it would be a good idea if I rang his practice and made an appointment to come and see him - just like I did last month and the month before that.

Finders Weepers

When the first three lottery balls dropped out of Saturday night's rolling drum Elspeth wasn't paying attention. She didn't even hear the inanely enthusiastic voice of the TV announcer introducing them. Instead she had one eye on an article in a magazine about breast-feeding and one eye on the toenail she was carefully stroking Pink Amazon polish onto.

She'd decided to do her toenails on a whim because she'd heard earlier that day from a young mother who came into the café where she worked that it wouldn't be long before she wouldn't even be able to see her toenails without standing in front of a mirror, let alone reach them. The magazine article had caught her eye because, although Elspeth had every intention of breast-feeding her baby when it arrived, a couple of quotes from the testimonies from celebrities about sore nipples and unsightly leaking concerned her. She just wanted to be sure she had all the facts. Her baby was still seven months away but time was going so quickly and there was so much still to learn. As if readying herself for the constant responsibility that a baby brings, she already spoke to it as though it were another person in the room.

Beside her on the arm of the sofa sat a lottery ticket, an insignificant little square of paper that had cost £1 to buy and which had on it a single line of numbers.

The machine in the TV studio selected the fourth ball and the man announced it. It was 17. This time Elspeth did glance up. She checked the numbers on the ticket and 17 was there. She didn't give it too much thought but she watched to see what the next number would be.

It was 38.

Elspeth checked the ticket. 38 was there too. She then quickly checked the three numbers that had already come up, the three she had missed and her eyes flitted between the ticket and the TV as though she were watching a speeded up game of tennis. Ticket. TV. Ticket. TV. Up. Down. Up. Down. Incredibly, she had four of the five numbers called and all of a sudden the TV had her undivided attention. She uncurled her legs, placed the nail polish on the floor, grabbed the ticket and perched herself on the edge of sofa in one rapid, fluid movement. The drum in the TV studio continued spinning, the coloured balls inside it dancing like butterflies in a washing machine. Elspeth's pulse quickened. The sixth ball dropped down and ran along the short tube to join its chosen companions. It was 35. Elspeth checked the ticket in her hand. 35 was there. It was the second to last number in the line. She let out an involuntary squeal but pulled it back when the announcer introduced the imminent arrival of the bonus ball.

It arrived. It was number 2.

Although Elspeth hadn't chosen the numbers herself, she had looked at them several times by now and she was fairly certain that she'd see the number 2. She checked anyway.

It was there. It was the first number in the line.

Her pulse raced. The TV graphics sorted the balls into ascending numerical order, just like they were on the ticket and the announcer counted them out clearly and concisely.

5 – 6 – 14 – 17 – 35 – 38 – and tonight's bonus ball – 2.

Again Elspeth's eyes darted from the ticket to the screen. Up and down. Just to be sure she was seeing correctly. She then leapt into the air with both arms outstretched and squealed again, louder this time, something between a Yippee! and a Yikes!

A short time later, her husband, Richard, returned. He was carrying a plastic bag of Chinese takeaway and he was dripping wet.

'Jesus! It's chucking it down out there,' he whined, dropping the bag on the doormat and kicking the door closed with the heel of a foot. The entrance to their little flat opened directly onto the living room, which had a compact but sadly, rather battered kitchenette built into one corner. Elspeth was on the sofa. Her back was to him. The TV screen was blank.

'Sorry Sweets but I didn't have enough for the spring rolls. They did give us some prawn crackers on the house though,' he said, shaking off his sodden leather jacket, which he hung over a hook on the back of the door.

'That was nice of them,' replied Elspeth, trying to keep her voice from quivering with excitement. Richard began prising off his wet trainers without bending down but he must have noticed her unusually sober tone.

'El. You ok?'

She didn't respond. She was itching to explode all over him with the news of their amazing stroke of luck but she wanted the moment to last just a little longer.

'El? What's up?' He kicked his trainers off and took a step towards her but it was more than Elspeth could stand. She couldn't contain the joy any longer and it breached her playful act like a might of water finally breaking through a fissure in a concrete dam. She jumped off the sofa and spun around to face her, by now, mildly concerned husband. He took a step a back, clearly startled by her sudden movement.

'You'll never guess what?' she cried.

'Oh my God, don't do that. You had me worried there for a moment,' he replied, hand on chest. 'What's happened?'

'Guess.'

He looked around the room for a clue as to what she was on about but seconds later he shrugged.

'I give up.'

Elspeth rushed around the sofa to him, her face beaming.

'My God El. What's up?'

She produced the lottery ticket from behind her back and thrust it towards his bewildered face. 'This,' she squealed, holding it so close to his eyes that he had to draw back to focus on it.

'What is it?' he asked.

'A lottery ticket,' she declared. 'A winning lottery ticket.'

'Oh yeah,' he said, rolling his eyes. 'How much did you win?' Neither of them had played the lottery before but they were both aware of how ridiculous the odds of winning were.

'See for yourself,' said Elspeth, reaching for the TV remote. She had rewound and then paused the lottery programme on their set-top box in preparation for his return and now as the screen flashed back to life, seven numbers in red circles hung frozen in the air, begging to be ogled. Richard took the ticket from Elspeth and regarded it with growing interest. He compared the numbers on it to those on the screen.

'Is this a joke?' he asked, his eyes widening in alarm. 'A trick?'

'No.' Elspeth couldn't bring her voice down. It was at least an octave higher than usual.

'But, when did you....I mean, God El. This is amazing. You've got six of the numbers here.'

'I know. Five and the bonus.'

'But that's like...worth thousands, isn't it?'

'I know.'

'Jesus! This can't be real.'

'Look.' Elspeth took his hand and hustled him over to their laptop, which sat open on their small dining table by the kitchenette. The takeaway remained on the doormat, cooling and congealing in its foil trays, forgotten for the moment.

Elspeth brushed a finger across the trackpad and the screensaver vanished, replaced by the prize breakdown page of the National Lottery website. She pointed to the line that revealed the winnings for tonight's five plus the bonus and began flapping her arms with excitement.

Five winners had an equal share of £1,108,841.

'Two hundred and twenty one thousand, seven hundred and sixty eight pounds,' read Richard from the next column, indicating how much each winner would receive.

'I know,' squealed Elspeth. 'It's amazing.'

'It is,' replied a slightly confused Richard. 'Amazing.' He was still staring at the computer screen when she saw it finally dawn on him and when he turned and saw her flapping and squealing beside him he began flapping and squealing as well until they were both jumping up and down like children on a trampoline.

'You know what this means?' Richard asked.

'Yes,' shrieked Elspeth. 'We're rich!' She squealed again and Richard joined in with his own flatter, deeper squeal that harmonised quite well with her ear-piercing note. Then they both burst out laughing, real unadulterated, careless, reckless laughter that came from deep within their hearts. They hugged and jumped and kissed, two people lost together in a moment of pure bliss.

'But, hey! Be careful,' gasped Richard, bringing their crazy celebratory dance to a gentle stop. He placed a tender hand on the slight swelling of her stomach and Elspeth felt as though she had never been, nor could she ever be happier.

Eventually, they managed to bring their bubbling ecstasy down to a lively simmer and this allowed them to remember they had bought takeaway. After reheating it in the microwave, they sat down at the little table to eat. For a while, they sat in silence, consuming the food with little of the enthusiasm with which it was ordered. It was approaching eleven o'clock now and they were both being overtaken with fatigue, particularly Elspeth who was drained all the time anyway on account of her energy fuelling the growth of another person inside her womb. They were silent too, imagining what their future would now look like with this significant windfall to boost their finances.

Getting a place of their own was the top priority. Renting was so hideously expensive and what their money was getting them at the moment was far from ideal. Their flat above a charity shop in the high street had only one bedroom and with a child on the way, a second room was quite simply, a necessity. It was also a cluttered flat due to a complete lack of storage space and the bathroom suffered from condensation and mildew. Their own home with a manageable mortgage in a nicer area was their dream and with two hundred grand in the bank, it was a possibility. So was a newer car and maybe even a short holiday, a last fling somewhere alone together before their two became three. Generally providing for little Nathan or little Molly when he or she arrived would now be less of a financial struggle and that was a huge relief to them both. It would mean that Elspeth wouldn't have to rush back into another job and that Richard, a resting actor and reluctant waiter, might not have to rely on so much overtime.

Later as they lay in bed they were too wired to sleep. The call to the lottery hotline first thing in the morning had them itching for the sun to rise. They were deliriously happy, their spirits buoyed by their unexpected elation and they amused themselves for several hours talking and laughing about what the money would do for them. Eventually their overwhelming tiredness began to quieten their minds and their animated voices decreased into croaky whispers. The torpid presence of sleep was finally in the room. The curtains across the window were dark and heavy and did a good job of keeping out the light from the street but they didn't create an absolute seal. A rectangle of orange glow surrounded them and gave the room indefinable shadows. After a while, Richard's hoarse whisper broke the silence.

'Sweets? What made you to buy a ticket? You never have before. Seems like such a random thing to do. Almost as if you knew you were going to win.'

Elspeth nearly didn't answer. She was drifting towards the river of dreams. Her eyelids were leaden.

'I didn't buy it,' she replied after a while. 'One of our customers dropped it.'

'Huh?'

Another pause.

'I didn't buy it. A customer dropped it under a table.'

'Oh God. How gutting must that be?'

'Yeah, must be kicking himself. Poor sod.' She said it half mumbling, half chuckling. For several minutes the silence returned and then Elspeth heard Richard call her name as if from a distance.

'Elspeth?'

Sleep was very nearly upon her but something in his tone pulled her back from the brink. He never normally used her full name unless they were arguing or if someone had died.

'Hmm?'

'You didn't see who dropped it, did you?'

'Yeah, it was that Edwin guy.'

Suddenly the room was aglow with honeyed light and even though Elspeth's eyes were closed, she instinctively squeezed them tighter. Richard had turned on his bedside light and sat up.

'Christ El! No. If you saw him drop it, don't you think you should have told him?' From out of nowhere, his tone had changed and become harsh, accusatory. 'Or given it back?'

'What? Why?' She was a little disoriented by his abrupt mood swing plus a little annoyed at having been drawn back from the precipice of glorious slumber. She turned onto her side away from him and mumbled, 'Haven't you heard of finders keepers?'

'But you didn't find it. You saw someone drop it. There's a difference.'

'How is there a difference?' she said, rolling onto her back again and squinting at him. 'I saw something on the floor and I picked it up. Like I said, finders keepers. It's not like it was worth anything at the time. Ok, it was worth a pound. Maybe I'll give the guy a pound when he's next in.'

'Jesus El, you cannot be serious? It's stealing and you know it.'

Elspeth took a deep breath. She was moments away from sleep and now this.

'How is it? It's not like I took it from him.'

'You might as well have. You were one step away from picking the man's pocket! What about if he'd dropped his wallet? Would you have kept that too? I don't think so.'

'Of course not! Oh Richard, go to sleep. The ticket's ours now and we're collecting the prize so stop thinking about how it came about. Call it chance. Call it luck. Perhaps I just happened to be in the right place at the right time. Whatever. He lost it. We found it. Simple as that.' She grabbed at the duvet and turned briskly away from him again.

'You're right. It is simple. You're giving it back. We have no right to that money.'

'What?' Elspeth couldn't believe her ears. She turned her head and regarded her husband with incredulity. 'And throw away everything we've spent the last how ever many hours talking about? Do you really want to do that Richard? Forget it. It's not going to happen.'

'Elspeth, for God's sake, listen to yourself. Where are you ethics?'

In her tired, annoyed state Elspeth's patience quickly ran out. She pushed herself up and turned to Richard.

'My ethics are buried somewhere beneath this rubble of a life we've built for ourselves. And all this damn hardship. And in a few months it's going to get a whole lot harder. What with the rent and the bills for this poxy little flat – that we both hate. Don't forget, I'm going to be out of a job soon for several months. At least! And we already know how much a childminder will cost when I go back to work. Not to mention the expenses of the baby's day-to-day needs. I mean, come on Richard. Can you honestly sit there and tell me you don't want this?' She placed a hand on his arm and softened her tone. 'We've been handed something amazing; let's not turn our noses up at it. We need this. You know we do.'

Richard breathed a sigh of uncertainty and slowly shook his head.

'You make it sound all right, but it's just not. Supposing they can find out if you're the person who bought the ticket. There's a bar code on it, you know? I'm sure they can trace it to an exact store and probably even an exact time. And what about Edwin? What if he knows the numbers? What if they're the same numbers he picks every week? Isn't it just a bit of a coincidence that we happen to win the same week?'

'So we don't tell him. We don't tell anybody.'

'Oh right. Suddenly we've just started earning enough to move house and buy a car!'

Elspeth hated it when her husband resorted to sarcasm and she'd often screamed at him for it but this time she let it go; she only wanted to soothe his concerns. 'We could've had savings. Or help from our parents. Or maybe we don't claim the money for a few weeks. Let the dust settle, so to speak.'

'I don't believe I'm hearing this. Ok, so you make the claim – whenever – and just to check it's your ticket, they ask you where you bought it. They'll know you know?'

'Oh for God's sake Richard. I don't know. Maybe I forgot. Maybe I bought it weeks ago on a busy shopping trip and I just can't remember. How can they check that? Stop worrying. Enjoy this miracle for what it is. It's our dream. To be able to live a little more comfortably. Come on.' She squeezed his shoulder with a pacifying hand and then rubbed his back with it.

When Richard didn't respond other than with a snort of contempt before turning off the light and pulling brusquely at the duvet, Elspeth thought she had won the battle. At times, her dear sweet husband could be too nice for his own good. Nothing more was said and yet as the time ticked by she could tell he wasn't sleeping. His breathing was too shallow and quiet and she could hear his head move on the pillow every now and again as if he were glancing across at her. She didn't want to set him off again on one of his 'holier than thou' crusades so she remained silent and tried to persuade sleep to come for her again.

What he had said though bothered her. She hadn't thought of it as stealing before but now that he had planted the seed, a feeling that she had done wrong began to spread through her euphoria like an unwanted creeper suffocating a blossoming rosebush.

She recalled the moment she had seen Edwin Turner drop the piece of paper as he stood up to leave the café. She was standing right beside his table having just given him his change. He stepped past her and she saw the ticket float down under the table out of sight. She immediately stooped to retrieve it but the impulse from her brain to call to him just didn't connect with her voice. She knew what it was she was reaching for and Edwin was less than ten feet away from her on his way out but she said nothing. Yes, she should have called out to him but she didn't. She couldn't. She didn't want to. Instead, she slipped the ticket into her apron pocket.

As she lay there in the dark attempting to defend her actions, a thought occurred to her. Sometimes in life we have to do things that might not appear to be completely honest. It's called surviving. Her fighting stance felt somehow appropriate with a child on the way and she knew she would probably be fighting for it for the rest of her life in one way or another. However, the gallant thought did little to halt the growing tendrils of guilt within her.

When morning came and Elspeth woke, the bed was all hers. This told her that Richard was still upset. Usually on a Sunday he'd enjoy a lay in while she made tea and got herself ready for a morning in the café. Then, while she was at work he'd do their weekly shop in town before coming home and preparing lunch for her return. Sunday afternoon was generally the most peaceful and relaxing time of their week and if the weather allowed and they could be bothered, they would often blow the cobwebs away with a walk along the seafront; though since being pregnant she hadn't had the energy for much else outside of work.

Richard was sitting on the sofa, head in the laptop when she went in to make her tea. The sweet, oily smell from last night's takeaway lingered in the room despite the window being ajar and a cool breeze blowing in. It was still raining heavily outside and the noise of a million droplets of water smattering onto the street sounded like a large crowd applauding a little way off.

Elspeth still felt guilty despite her best efforts to curtail it with the scythe of self-interest. She accepted that what she had done was probably wrong but at the same time, it was a situation that nobody else would ever need to know about. With this in mind, a large part of her wished she had lied to Richard last night and simply told him she'd bought the ticket; that way no one else but her would have to live with the guilt - a guilt she probably wouldn't even be feeling. But what's done is done and for her, two hundred thousand pounds was worth a little guilt if it meant a better life. She would have no trouble living with it even if Richard couldn't. But she knew that his moral sensibilities would need massaging in order for him to accept the situation her way and so she'd decided that in order for him to be able to do this, it would be necessary for them to delay their claim for at least a few weeks. It would probably be a wise precaution too just in case he was right about the lottery people checking up on them. She was sure she'd heard somewhere that winners were still able to claim their prizes for a year or so after the draw however, she'd have to check to be certain.

'Morning,' she said, with an optimistic air as she filled the kettle. 'How long you been up?'

'A while.' Richard's tone was as cool as the draught that came in through the window. He got up and joined her by the sink with the laptop open in his hands. 'Something here I think you should read.' He had highlighted a section of the National Lottery's website.

'Oh for goodness…'

'Read it!' he snapped. Elspeth didn't want a rerun of last night's argument so she read the highlighted text. It was in the FAQ section and it stated that if you found a ticket before the 180-day claim period (oh well, at least that clears that up) without the owner's name on it or if you were unable to return it to its rightful owner then you should send it to lottery HQ. If thereafter, the ticket remained unclaimed by its rightful owner within the 180 days, you may, at the company's discretion, receive the prize.

Richard also showed her a paragraph intended for those who had lost their ticket and it stated that the owner could still make a claim and that upon successful checking of the facts, the prize could still be given out.

'So don't you think it stands to reason that with everything being done on computers, records are easy to access and they will do some checking? Particularly with the amount of money involved. And if Edwin makes a claim as well and they check and find that he did actually buy the damn thing, we'll be right in the shit! God El, I wish you hadn't been so bloody stupid. What were you thinking?'

'How about we wait a while?' reasoned Elspeth. She wasn't about to give up her dream so easily, despite the sense of impending loss that was bearing down on her optimism like a balloon under a seat cushion. 'Let's see what Edwin does. Maybe he won't remember he had a ticket. Maybe they were random numbers and he doesn't know he's won. Or maybe even, it wasn't his. Maybe he found it and so he's not even bothered he lost it.'

'You really are clutching at straws El. Maybe he died in his sleep last night and so nobody will ever know he bought the ticket.'

Richard moved back to the sofa and sat down. Elspeth spooned the teabag out of her mug and flicked it aggressively into the sink. God, she hated his sarcasm. The atmosphere in the room couldn't have been more different from the previous night.

Richard's accusing glare encouraged her to leave for work earlier than usual. He was also giving her the silent treatment, which absolutely infuriated her. The rain, coming down more like galvanized nails than droplets of water persuaded her to take a bus rather than walk the ten minutes to the café. With Elspeth living just up the road, it was usually down to her to arrive early and set up. This was fine by her because it was a gentle start to the morning's work and simply involved turning everything on and taking chairs off tables where they had been put the night before to aid cleaning the floor. Restocking the pre-packaged snacks on display was also part of her early routine. Angela, her boss and owner of the café, would arrive just before opening time with a carload of freshly baked cakes and buns, which they would transfer to the counter displays or to the fridges for when they were needed.

Elspeth got off the bus and, huddled beneath the inadequate span of her umbrella, hurried across the saturated road to the café. As she fumbled in her handbag for the keys, she noticed a tall, skinny figure under a black umbrella hovering outside the door. She knew immediately who it was. She didn't need to see his face or recognise his lanky proportions. It was Edwin Turner. Her heart told her so.

Her footsteps faltered as a mushroom of dread sprang up from the pit of her stomach and into her throat. He strode towards her, intercepting her before she reached the door.

'Elspeth. Morning.' She barely knew the man other than by name but one thing she liked about him was the way he spoke. He was always terribly polite to the point that he came across as borderline insincere. But this morning there was a bluntness in his voice that was uncharacteristic. He came into the café about twice a week and always made a cappuccino and a chocolate muffin last almost two hours. Elspeth often wondered what he did for a living as he was always shabbily dressed in V-neck pullovers and old corduroys with elbow patches, like an old teacher out of mothballs, and he never failed to appear exhausted. But today his face looked even more haggard than normal and behind the high collar of his Inspector Columbo raincoat Elspeth could see his eyes were red-ringed as though he'd been crying. His miserable countenance did nothing to help her composure but she ordered herself to be resolute.

'Hi Edwin.' They had to talk louder than normal due to the drumming of the rain on their umbrellas. Elspeth suddenly decided to be extremely busy. That way she'd have no time for chitchat, especially that of the unwanted kind. 'I'm sorry but we aren't open 'til ten.'

'I know but…'

'Can this wait then?' she interrupted, as she put the key in the door. 'I've got loads…'

But Edwin cut her off. 'I just wanted to ask if anyone handed in a lottery ticket yesterday afternoon or if you'd found one when you cleared up last night.'

'A what?' Elspeth nearly choked on her reply. Her heart seemed to be obstructing her throat, which in turn was hampering the movement of her tongue. She pushed open the door, lowered her umbrella and stepped inside.

'A lottery ticket. You know?' Edwin stayed out in the rain.

'Um,' Elspeth knew this was it. The point of no return. The line in the sand. The moment to tell the truth or to maintain the lie. Which was it to be? Come clean and make this man's day? Or continue to covet two hundred thousand pounds that wasn't rightfully hers? Right or wrong? Good or bad? 'No, n…not that I know of,' she stuttered, stunning herself with the words. Until a second ago, she had been leaning towards handing over the ticket, through want of putting an end to the doubt and the guilt that had amassed within her since her argument with Richard last night. She was after all a good person - at least she thought she was - and she didn't really want to squander her integrity. But the lure of this magnificent windfall was too great to resist and she heard herself lying to him. Then she started to babble. 'But then I didn't do the clearing up yesterday. I left before it was...I mean Angela did the um...so I'll ask...she'll be here in a while and it's...I'll ask her and see if she knows anything.' She felt stupid and embarrassed and was sure her cheeks were signalling her guilt like red warning lights.

'Do you mind if I come in and look around?' asked Edwin, taking a step forward. 'Please. Just in case. You see, we won last night.' His lips became a thin, grave line and his voice took on the guttural quality of someone in deep despair. 'But I lost the ticket.'

The rain persisted all morning. Gutters from two and three stories high, unable to cope with the volume of rainwater running down the roofs, overflowed their burdens in splattering columns onto the pavements and awnings of the shop fronts below. Kerbside drains became submerged beneath slowly expanding puddles around which pedestrians sidestepped to avoid getting splashed by the traffic.

Elspeth returned home a little later than usual. Despite the weather she'd walked back and quite simply got soaked. The aroma of a roast lunch met her on the stairs and, where it would normally have set her mouth watering and her stomach rumbling, today it did nothing of the sort. Her appetite was zero.

Richard was turning potatoes in the roasting pan when she entered. She closed the door and stood, listless and dripping like a woollen pullover on a washing line. The flat depressed her, even more so today. The boxes of books stacked against a wall because there was no space to take them out. The sagging column of bin liners piled up in a corner, each one filled with summer clothes that had no cupboard space to call their own. Suddenly she burst out crying.

'Oh my God, El. What's up?' said Richard as he thrust the pan back into the oven and rushed over to her.

'I'm sorry,' she cried, as she leaned into his shoulder.

'Aww, I'm sorry too. I hate it when we fight.' He hugged her to his chest and patted her sodden back as they continued mumbling apologies to each other. Then he said, 'Come on, let's get you out of these wet things.'

'I gave the ticket back,' she sniffed. 'So you don't have to be mad at me anymore.'

'Did you really?' Richard took her coat and hung it up. 'Well, you did the right thing and I'm proud of you.' He hugged her again but she howled and her tears streamed down onto his shoulder. 'I know. I know,' he said, patting her back. 'For a moment there, it felt great being rich, didn't it?'

Her sobbing continued but she managed to say between stuttering gasps, 'I don't know why...I'm being so silly about this. I just...really wanted things to be better for us...and the baby.'

'They will El. They will. Come on, off with your boots.' He helped her out of them and walked her to the sofa. The bottom half of her jeans were wet but she didn't care. 'So old Edwin came in looking for it did he? What did he say?'

'I think maybe that's why...I'm so upset,' she admitted, reaching for a box of tissues. 'Oh Richard. How could I have even considered being so heartless, so awful? What's wrong with me?'

'Come on El. In the end you didn't do anything wrong. It was just a naughty thought and we all have those from time to time. You were just thinking of our child and the environment it's coming into.'

She began sobbing again but after a few minutes, when she had calmed herself, Richard urged her to tell him what had happened with Edwin Turner.

'He was there outside the shop waiting for me,' she began. 'And even when he asked me to my face if I'd seen his ticket, I lied to him. How could I?'

'Ok. Enough now. Carry on.'

'He wanted to come in and look around himself and I let him but then he just broke down and told me all about his daughter and about how she's going to die unless she can go to America and have an operation that costs thousands of pounds.'

'Really?'

'He said he's been doing the lottery with the vain hope that he'd win because he said it was the only option left to him now. Apparently, she was born with some spinal defect that affects the growth of her brain and although she's able to live a reasonably normal life, go to school and that, she needs daily care and drugs to help with the pain. He said he's already remortgaged his house to pay for her ongoing medical bills so unless Fate lends a hand, she's probably going to die within a year. I didn't realise this but he said he made an appeal for local donations several months ago, but he said it didn't raise anywhere near enough. Oh that poor little girl.' She placed a hand on her stomach and thought of her own little person growing inside. 'Can you imagine being so utterly helpless that you're forced to put your faith in such ridiculous odds? Richard, supposing we have to face something like that? What would we do? Anyway, that's why I gave him the ticket. Because he needs it far, far more than we do. And I really don't want that bad karma following me everywhere and affecting those I love.' She curled a hand behind his neck and pulled his face to her lips. 'I'm so sorry.'

'So you just gave it to him?'

'I pretended that it got thrown out with the rubbish.' She sniffed and dried her puffy eyes on a clean tissue. A feeble smile twitched across her face like a streak of lightening crawling across the sky as she remembered the moment she made the man's day. 'You should've seen the look on his face Richard. It was indescribable really. I've never seen anyone so relieved. He told me that I'd saved his daughter's life but I don't think I did. If I'd had my way, if you hadn't convinced me I was doing wrong, I would've been responsible for killing her.' Suddenly she broke down again and wept as though the child had already died at her hand.

'Hey, hey, come on,' said Richard, pulling her towards him again and holding her tight. 'There's no need for this. And I'll tell you why. Edwin Turner doesn't have a daughter.' The words took a few seconds to sink in.

'What?' Elspeth's tear-soaked eyes followed Richard as he got up and moved to the window. 'What do you mean, he doesn't have a daughter?'

Richard paused a moment before turning back and when he did his expression was bleak.

'A couple of the guys in the restaurant know him. I've heard them speak about him. He doesn't have a daughter. Or any child for that matter. In fact he doesn't even have a wife.' He moved gloomily across to the cooker and ignited a flame under a couple of saucepans. 'He lives at home with his decrepit old mum in a council house down near the old bus depot.'

'But…'

'Forget it El.'

Weird Vibrations

The iron kissing-gate clangs against its stop behind us, its rusty hinges squealing out for a drop of oil. As usual, it sets my teeth on edge and as usual I think about fixing it tomorrow with a squirt of '3 in 1'. It doesn't seem to bother the choir of grasshoppers performing in the surrounding long grass though so I reckon if they can put up with it, so can I. Besides, this walk, this path with its scenery, its sounds and smells has been a part of my day for longer than I can remember and I'd probably miss the sound if the hinges were oiled.

Spencer is impatient for his nightly run through the woods behind the vicarage and is straining against his leash. As usual when he's dying to get away from me, his breathing comes in a sort of wheeze from the back of his throat as though he's being throttled. It sounds painful and I often wonder if it hurts him but I guess it doesn't or he wouldn't pull so hard.

I've no doubt that if he could talk, he'd tell me that this is his favourite part of our evening walk; the chance for him to end the day on a high by revelling in a brief moment of wild abandon, of giving in to instinct and experiencing a few minutes away from the leash and the domesticity handed down to him through generations. The feverish anticipation he shows as we turn into the alleyway that leads us here is a clear sign that he's about to wallow in a moment of pure dog euphoria. He knows his routine and that all too soon, he'll be back home wolfing down his dinner as though he's got a bus to catch. Then they'll be nothing left for him to do but to curl up in front of the hearth for the night to dream perhaps of chasing cats and rabbits, It's no wonder he's excited to make the most of these last few moments outside. Bless him.

I unclip his lead and he shoots off like a greyhound powering out from a racing trap. Within seconds, he's bounded into the waist high grass of the meadow and disappeared from view. It's the same thing every time we come here and I marvel that he never grows bored of running through the same patch. I guess that's the beauty of it, to be content with such a simple thing, a simple pleasure. Oh yes, it's a dog's life all right.

I head down the path towards the woods that back onto the graveyard and I'm in no rush; it's such a lovely evening. There isn't a breath of wind and it's warm enough that I'm not wearing a cardigan, just the short-sleeved cotton dress that I ordered from the catalogue a couple of months ago.

The air here is filled with the constant chitter chatter of hedgerow birds readying themselves for the night and somewhere nearby a blackbird sings its glorious heart out from a treetop in response to another a little further off. Whatever they're saying to each other, it's absolutely beautiful. I stop to smell a candyfloss-pink flower on a dog rose that seems to be scrambling with some success up and over a high hedge, which itself seems to have grown quite well around the ancient iron railings that mark the boundary of the church's land. The rose's sweet, delicate scent is pure summer, clean and fresh and natural and even better than freshly laundered bed sheets dried on the line. And that's saying something.

It won't be long before the hedgerows that crisscross the fields here are blanketed with ripe blackberries and I know for a fact that my boys will be pleading with me to get out and start picking so I can make their favourite tarts and crumbles. For a brief moment, I consider asking them if they'd like to help me pick a bowl or two themselves this year but then their answer comes to me like a psychic vision from the future. 'Huh, fat chance, Mum!' The thought makes me smile. Anyway, I don't mind doing it. I find it quite satisfying, picking my own fruit.

Above me, the evening star stands alone and friendless in the vast expanse of cloudless sky, the colours of which are a cool range of blues and violets. The sun is now well below the horizon and darkness is coming on quickly but for the moment, it's still possible to see without my torch. However, as the path leads me into the shroud of the trees, I switch it on and its bright beam spreads a white oval on the ground in front of me.

Somewhere off to my left among the dark shadows of bracken and brambles I hear Spencer running amok, his paws snapping twigs as he runs through the undergrowth with an eyesight far superior to my own. Incredibly, even though he seems lost in his own little world, chasing unseen creatures and following intriguing scents backwards and forwards, his nose brushing the ground like the end of a vacuum hose, he always seems to keep up with me, instinctively tied to my flank via an invisible thread of dependency or protection, I'm not sure which.

All of a sudden my ears pop like they do when I'm on a train entering a tunnel at full speed. I swallow to counter the effect and they clear but all I hear then is the flip-flopping of my sandals on the hard dry earth. There's no other sound. Intrigued by the silence I stop walking. A strange hush seems to have descended all around as if the evening is holding its breath. Then, as I wonder where all the grasshoppers and birds have gone, I hear a strange hum, quite faint and probably a long way off. It's something like the sound an electricity sub-station makes, only not constant; it seems to rise and fall rhythmically, like a mechanical heartbeat.

It's a sound I find difficult to put my finger on because it's as unfamiliar and yet as noticeable as would be the lack of any squeal if the iron hinges on the gate were oiled. I shrug it off as nothing more than a sound I haven't heard before and carry on walking but then after a few paces I stop again. I've walked this path often enough year round to recognise all the usual noises, no matter what's going on around the village but this sound is definitely a new one to me. I know that the nearest building is the vicarage and yet from where I'm standing I reason that the vicarage should be well out of earshot. Or maybe it isn't on a perfectly still evening like this. And yet if it is coming from there, what could be making such a sound? It's not a lawnmower and certainly not a car and the closest electricity pylon is at least a mile away.

And so together with the fact that I'm in a dark wood and just a stone's throw from several hundred lichen-covered gravestones, I feel unnerved and I call for Spencer to come to me. But Spencer is already beside me sitting timidly at my feet as though I've told him off for stealing food or pooping on the carpet. His tongue lolls in and out the side of his mouth like a thick slice of boiled ham.

'Good boy,' I say, kneeling down and stroking the top of his smooth golden head. 'What's up then? What brings you back so soon?' He usually doesn't catch up with me until we're free of the woods and heading up towards the rear of the vicarage and even then, I often have to call him to me. In the light of the torch, his soft brown eyes seem to appeal to me for reassurance and when I pat the side of his neck he pushes his nose under my arm as though to shield himself from something. 'What is it Spence? What do you see?' Of course, if he could talk he'd tell me but he can't so he just sits there, panting with his ears pricked up at the odd sound that doesn't seem to be coming from any one direction in particular. I tell him (and myself) that it's probably just a farmer working in a nearby field, his tractor droning up and down a line of wheat. But I know very well what that sounds like and so I'm far from convinced.

'Come on then,' I say, standing up and setting off down the path. 'Let's get you back for your dinner.' I realise how suddenly eager I am to get home and I tell myself that my nerves are surely jangling too much over a silly hum. But to be honest, I feel uneasy.

Instead of following though, Spencer remains where his is and lets out a little whimper. It then dawns on me that he's probably picked up a thorn in one of his paws - something that has happened before and would certainly explain his wounded manner - but as I go back and bend down to check him over, the torch goes out and we're swallowed up by the darkness. I give the torch a good shake and bang the side of its plastic body against my palm but it doesn't come back on.

'Oh, damn. I don't believe it!'

I stand up and peer through the inky blackness, trying to force my eyes to find the path that will lead us out of the wood, around the edge of the field that skirts the vicarage and then take us back up to the main road. But it's too dark under these trees to even see the pale coat of the dog at my feet.

It then occurs to me that Spencer's eyes being better than mine, means he can probably lead the way out of the wood, like a sort of untrained guide dog for someone who's temporarily blind. I reach down with searching hands and fumble in the pitch dark to reattach the leash to his collar. But then the odd humming sound becomes an even odder vibration within my body and I find myself unable to move. My heartbeat quickens and my throat becomes dry as jangling nerves swell into fear. I wonder if I'm having a heart attack or some other kind of seizure and I try to move forward to get home or at least to the vicarage - there's no one to help me here - but I can't. A strong smell of what I can only describe as warm metal fills the air and I hear Spencer whimpering at my feet like he does during a thunderstorm.

All of a sudden, a blinding light comes down through the canopy of trees and encircles me like an actor onstage beneath a spotlight. Only this is much, much brighter. I'm absolutely petrified. The beam is too intense to look up into to see where it's coming from yet I can't hear anything above me. I can't hear anything but the distant humming sound that also seems to resonate in my bones.

The dazzling light vanishes as abruptly as it appeared and as I stand there trying to make sense of what it could have been – a helicopter? a firework? a flare? - I notice the torch is working again only it's on the floor throwing a long cone of light up the path and not in my hand. Assuming I must have dropped it in my panic, I reach down to pick it up and am instantly aware that both the metallic smell and the distant hum have gone, though my body seems to retain a certain tingle from those vibrations. My relief is so great it makes me feels weak but I'm still on full alert and my heart is still thumping against my ribs.

Then, I notice Spencer isn't at my feet.

'Spencer!' Here boy! Spencer!' I swing the beam around, searching the darkness, whistling and calling for him as I start off down the path towards home, my pace somewhat quicker than before. I shiver briefly at the realisation that it has got a little chilly and I can feel a tightening of my skin as goose bumps break out on my arms and legs. Before I have gone a dozen steps, the dog appears on the path ahead of me, his head held low, tail wagging at half speed as he trots towards me, the leash dragging between his front paws.

'There you are boy. Where did you go? Were you scared? Ah, come here.' I kneel down and give him a good pet before carrying on homewards, all the while trying to rationalise the light - a toy airplane? a new fangled piece of farming equipment?

Ten minutes later, I step into my kitchen and feel the warmth of the stove embrace me. I call to my husband that there's something I want to ask him. Maybe he'll know what's going on outside. I hear him heave himself out of his armchair and call back to me as he heads down the hall.

'There you are,' he says, as I shut the door behind me and replace the torch on the windowsill. 'Who you been nattering to then?' He adds, turning on the tap to fill the kettle.

'Nobody,' I reply, hanging Spencer's lead on the hook beside the door.

'Well, what kept you?'

I glance at the clock on the wall but have to double-check it against the one on the cooker. The twenty-minute circle that Spencer and I have just completed, the same one we do most evenings when the weather is fine has somehow taken us almost an hour and a half.

The Christmas Box

'There you are, m'love,' said Mrs Ashcroft, producing several coins from a pocket in her thick woollen cardigan. The brown and white Collie at her feet was sniffing keenly at Toby's boots and as she lent forward to restrain the animal, the overhead porch light cast a ghoulish shadow over her face.

'Thank you,' replied Toby, swapping the money for a neatly folded Evening Echo. Silvery veils of breath curled around their heads and drifted gently up towards the light.

'You'll be calling next week?' she asked. 'Last Friday before Christmas n'all, I want to give you a little something extra.'

'Thanks Mrs Ashcroft,' he answered, blue eyes twinkling. 'Yeah, I'll be calling as usual. But don't forget there's no paper next Saturday or the Monday after.' Toby smiled at the thought; he was looking forward to two evenings off.

'Yes, I got your little note and that's fine.' She tucked the newspaper under her arm. 'Now, don't you go dithering about on a night like this. You'll catch your death. Well, goodbye.'

Toby assured her that he most certainly would not be dithering about and thanked her again. She smiled at his politeness and, pulling the dog inside, closed the door. Toby pocketed the coins and retreated carefully up the icy path. He didn't count the money because he didn't need to. Mrs Ashcroft was clearly a woman of habit and in the eight months and three weeks since Toby had taken over the paper round from his older brother, her weekly payment had always been the same – sixty pence for the papers and fifteen pence for him. It wasn't much by way of a tip but it was more than some gave. He squeezed himself between the broken gate and the holly hedge and with an effort that shook the hoary frosting from the bushes he yanked the gate shut. The porch light blinked out and Toby found himself once again alone with his shadow in the crystalline moonlight. One down, sixteen to go.

Friday was Toby's best and worst day on his paper-round. On the one hand, it was payday and he would pocket around three pounds in tips but on the other, Friday's paper included a classified section, which made each one twice as thick as usual; and twice as thick meant twice as heavy. Until he was well into the round, the strap of his sack would dig annoyingly into his shoulder.

The day had been cloudless with a faded denim sky and around noon the previous day's snowfall had begun to thaw. However, as the afternoon wore on and darkness began its early wintertime descent, the temperature had fallen with it encrusting the ground with a stony frost. Beneath the vivid brilliance of a waxing moon, the village and surrounding countryside glistened as though dusted with sugar.

Every day for the last week, the gritting lorry had been toing and froing, spreading its rust-coloured crumble along the main street but patches of ice on the pavement crunched like broken bottles beneath Toby's boots. He crossed the road in front of the school where earlier that afternoon the younger children of the village had been boisterously making festive decorations and hanging them from the walls and ceilings of their classrooms. Now though, the school was silent and empty apart from Mrs Funnell, the caretaker, who would be busy emptying bins and sweeping up the spilt glitter and silver stars.

Toby made his way towards his next stop behind the school playing fields. The strap of the paper sack already pained his shoulder and as he hefted it onto his other side to relieve the discomfort, he stepped onto a mirror of ice and his right boot shot forwards. He collapsed heavily onto his backside with his left foot twisting awkwardly beneath him and let out a cry of frustration. He hated doing his paper-round on foot but ever since a pedal had snapped off his old bicycle he had been left with no choice. His mother, who spent her mornings scrubbing and dusting at several of the village's larger households, had told him she couldn't afford a replacement and so he had begun the lengthy endeavour of saving for one himself. He had even set his heart on a particular model – the new Road Warrior 5000 with a three speed twisting handgrip and side-stand. But as the weeks went by and his savings grew at a pitiful rate - not helped by his passion for toffee Bonbons - he realised that it would take several years to save enough for the bike of his dreams. Toby unfolded himself from the ground and dusted himself off.

Outside of school, his friends in the village went everywhere on their bikes and for the last couple of months Toby had felt like a cowboy without a horse. And to top it all, his paper-round now took him three times as long. Whereas before, he would get it done straight after school and before tea, now he had to wait until after he had eaten (on his mother's request) and usually got home with little or no time to play before bedtime. Yes, not having a bike was a real nuisance.

He trudged on, taking extra care where the snow had been compacted into icy prints by earlier feet. Past the telephone box, across the little car park and through the open gate that marked the entrance to the playing fields. The row of cottages that overlooked the swings and slides was shrouded from the moonlight by a giant yew tree. Climbing its muscular boughs was one of Toby's favourite things to do during warmer months and from halfway up (the furthest he had dared yet reach), on a clear day he could see as far south as the Downs, nearly thirty miles distant.

Number four Parkside was in darkness but after several thuds with the heavy iron knocker, a light flicked on in the hallway. Through the frosted panes in the door, Toby could see the heavy figure of Mr Brown coming to greet him.

After the Browns, it was back across the main road and onto the new estate, the development's unofficial label enduring in the village despite it having been built two decades ago. But as it was the only major building the village had seen since the war it was still regarded as being recent. Made up of a cul-de-sac named Hillside View with two smaller cul-de-sacs - Oak Close and Birch Walk - shooting off from either side like the wings of a giant plane, it was where Toby would rid himself of the majority of his load. This was handy, because once down the bottom, it was a tough slog back up to the main road even with a half empty sack.

No weekly tip ever came from Mr Brown but Toby's next stop would be the most lucrative of his round. A nice crisp one-pound note would nestle alongside the sixty pence usually left for him in an envelope inside the letterbox affixed to the pale brickwork of the porch wall. Together with the new Mercedes in the driveway and the large fancy wreath pinned to the front door, Toby reckoned the Leslies were not short of a bob or two. Checking the contents of the envelope, he found a handwritten note reminding him they would be away from Wednesday of next week until the New Year and hoping that he had remembered to cancel their papers until then. It ended by saying 'A big thank you for delivering in all weathers' and wishing him a Merry Christmas. Folded neatly inside the note Toby found to his surprise and delight instead of a crisp one-pound note, a crisp five-pound note.

'Yes!' he cried, zipping it securely away inside his Parka. 'If everyone is as generous, I'll get my bike in no time.' But in truth Toby knew that not all of his money would be able to go towards his bike because he still had all of his Christmas shopping to do. He also had the vital expense of maintaining his supply of Bonbons. No, this unexpected fiver wouldn't be around for long.

His older brother Ralph, who had done the round for nearly two years before Toby, had said that Christmas was a good time for tips and that the previous year he had pocketed almost fifteen pounds extra. As much as that sounded when compared to his weekly pay, Toby knew he'd have to see quite a few

Christmases before he had enough for his bike. But as his best friend Ryan said - 'Every penny you get is a penny you didn't have,' - and for the most part Toby was a 'glass half full' sort of lad so for him, it was never too late to be disheartened.

One of Toby's customers along the main street had first mentioned his Christmas Box (as he liked to call it) back in early October and although he gave just ten pence extra each week, such was his enthusiasm when reminding Toby of it that Toby was expecting a tidy sum.

'I didn't get anything from the ol' codger last year so I wouldn't hold your breath,' Ralph had said disparagingly. 'Perhaps it'll actually be just an empty box for you to play with,' he had added with a teasing smirk.

Jim Worthingshaw, or ol' Jim, as he was affectionately known throughout the village, was an integral part of the community. Nobody seemed to know anything of his younger years, how old he was or where he was from; he was just there, resident at Number Two, The Street – a small unkempt red brick two up two down in a row of otherwise neat and tidy cottages. Usually, one would see him tramping around the village in shabby clothes, a cloth cap, an old hessian sack slung over one shoulder and a rolled cigarette dangling from his bottom lip. He would offer a cheerful greeting to anyone and everyone, would always doff his cap to a woman or girl and never missed a chance to stop and chat. He offered his services as gardener and handyman to anyone who would use them in Maydown Common and often rattled a wheelbarrow along with him filled with shears, spades and other gardening implements. This summer however people had commented on his noticeable absence and Toby had been told by his mother, who had overheard someone in the Post Office explain, that ol' Jim's sister, who shared the little cottage with him, had passed away.

Toby had felt an instant empathy for the old man, knowing only too well the heartache of losing a family member. His own father had died suddenly three years ago having returned home from work one day complaining of a headache. He had taken himself off to bed early without eating his tea and fallen straight asleep but when Toby's mother had turned in for the night a few hours later, she found her husband cold and lifeless. Toby had been overwhelmed with a sense of abandonment and confusion and had felt a desperate need to talk to somebody but his friends were too young to understand and his mother had insisted he be grown up about it and not need mollycoddling. Ralph had turned quiet and moody and began to spend more and more time with his friends or fishing by himself - his latest hobby - and so reluctantly, Toby had kept his feelings to himself.

Having the loss of a loved one in common seemed to bridge the years between Toby and Jim and it quickly became a routine that whilst delivering his paper, Toby would pop in and have a little chat with the old man. They spoke of everything from Toby's schoolteachers and the benefit of a good spin bowler in the side to the best time to plant carrots and how many broken bones each had suffered. They had even spoken of their losses, Jim mostly unwilling and guarded but Toby releasing his innermost feelings like a long overdue confession. In Jim, he had found a suitable sounding board for his troubles and it had felt good to finally talk to someone who understood what he'd been through.

His mother was not so approving of his visits to Number Two.

'Leave him alone and let him have some peace,' she would say wrinkling her nose at the stench of cigarette smoke in Toby's clothes. But as the weeks went by, Toby began to value his newest friendship and so his visits continued. And on a freezing cold December evening he was very much looking forward to a cup of tea and a Bonbon or two in front of Jim's Rayburn.

It was business as usual in Oak Close and Birch Walk as Toby continued on his round and the sack gradually became less of a bother for his shoulder. The new estate was the only area of the village to have street lighting and this, together with the plastic salt boxes dotted around each cul-de-sac - an encouragement for residents to clear their own paths and pavements of ice - helped Toby stay off his backside.

When he said goodbye to the Marmadukes at number seventy-one - his last stop at the bottom of Hillside View - his feet were numb and his fingers were lobster pink, their tips smudged black with newspaper print. Unfortunately, as always when he had delivered to the Marmadukes, he then had to run the gauntlet back past number sixty-three - home to possibly the most unpleasant kids in the whole of Maydown Common. The Craigs had three daughters between the ages of six and eleven and for some reason they delighted in teasing him relentlessly as he went by their house. And the taunting was always the same, never more, never less.

Evenin' Echo…echo…echo…echo…' piped the trio of ginger haired girls from the upstairs windows as he hurried past on the opposite pavement. It was worse still during the warmer months when they were playing outside for they would follow him and tease him with their screeching voices until he was halfway up the hill. But locked away indoors on these cold wintry nights, the closest they could get to him was leaning out of their bedroom windows. Their shrill tormenting ended abruptly when a coarse voice from somewhere inside yelled - 'Shut them bloody windas!'

Like Mrs Ashcroft, many of Toby's customers said they wanted to give him a 'little something extra' next week. He did a quick calculation in his head based on assumptions and reckoned that including the fiver from the Leslies, he was likely to get somewhere in the region of fifteen pounds. A handy sum but unfortunately only a fraction of what he needed. But then he hadn't included ol' Jim.

Common sense told him the old man was unlikely to give much more than anyone else, and certainly not enough for a new bike and yet, Jim always spoke of his Christmas Box as though it would be something significant. But it just seemed too fantastic to believe particularly since he looked like a man who hardly had much to give away. Nevertheless, Toby chose to remain hopeful and couldn't stop thinking about what he might receive.

With just over a week to go until the big day, the cheer and goodwill that Toby encountered on his round heightened his excitement. Cosy hallways that he stood in while money was fetched were adorned with festive colour, greeting cards occupied every available space along walls and on ledges and if sitting room doors were left ajar, he often got a glimpse of a tree draped with tinsel and fairy lights. It all added to the magic.

He was looking forward to the arrival of his grandparents on Christmas Day who - barring more heavy snowfall - would be driving down from Surrey and staying for a few days. He was looking forward to pulling crackers and eating a wonderful turkey lunch but, like virtually every other child the world over, he was most looking forward to opening presents. Not surprisingly, money had featured prominently on his Christmas list this year but he was also hoping that he would get the Grand Prix racing set he had been asking for.

He was out of breath when he reached the main street again having run most of the way up Hillside View. This was partly to see off the cold and partly because he couldn't wait to get to Jim's to thaw out with a cuppa. His face felt raw, as though a thousand tiny needles were pricking it and the back of his throat burned with every breath.

Just four papers remained in the sack now but unfortunately for Toby one of them was the biggest nuisance of his entire round. It involved a fifteen-minute walk down dark and winding Weir Farm Lane to Douglas's Mill and if there was one delivery when Toby missed his bike more than any other, it was this one. But first, he had to deliver to the Horse and Groom, the vicarage and then ol' Jim. Usually he would leave his friend until last and accept his mug of tea as a reward for a job well done but tonight he was so cold that he considered it essential to defrost before making the half hour round trip down Weir

Farm Lane. After delivering to the pub's back door, and then slinking past the eerie elm trees in the churchyard, which were always scarier when the wind blew, Toby arrived at Jim's.

The old man usually took a while to open the door as he spent all of his time in the kitchen at the rear of the cottage. A heavy security bolt sliding across would signal his arrival and the solid door would be pulled open to reveal him in silhouette against the yellow glow from within. There was no porch light so how the old man recognised who was calling was a mystery but with a cough and a wheeze he would invite Toby in. This night however, Toby had to knock twice and when there was still no response, he peered through the letterbox to see the cottage was in darkness. Puzzled and slightly annoyed, he trudged down to Douglas's Mill mumbling softly that he'd probably die of hyperthermia on the way. Thirty minutes later, the cottage was still silent and so with a grunt of annoyance, Toby pushed the newspaper through the letterbox. This was the first time they had missed their evening chat and Toby went to sleep that night wondering where his elderly friend could have been.

'Sorry I missed ya last night,' said ol' Jim, his cigarette burning brightly as he drew on it between sentences. 'Had some business in Mayford and didn't get back 'til later. You all right?'

Mayford was the nearby town where Maydown Commoners went to do any personal business and shopping that couldn't be done in the village. It had a weekly market in the library car park where local producers sold things like cheeses and jams and vegetables and handmade curios and its high street was full of all the usual shops. The dentist and doctor's surgeries were both there and it was also where Toby went to school. The older children of Maydown Common would catch the bus from outside the primary school and travel the fifteen minutes north to Mayford Comprehensive.

'Yeah, I'm OK,' replied Toby, stepping into the musty warmth of the cottage. He had grown accustomed to the smoky fug that Jim lived in and where once it had made his eyes water and his throat sore, now he barely noticed it. 'But I missed me cuppa yesterday. I'm getting frostbite walking miles out there every night. What about you? I got worried when you weren't in.' Worried sounded better than annoyed, thought Toby.

'No need to worry 'bout me lad,' said Jim, closing the door. 'I tried to get back for ya but like I said, I had somethin' needed sortin' which took a bit longer 'n I thought. Go 'n warm up.'

Toby led the way into the kitchen and took off the sack, his gloves, hat, scarf and coat. He sat in an old pine chair and stretched out towards the soot stained Rayburn while Jim filled a teapot with boiling water. Snow started to thaw from his boots and pool around them in shiny spots on the bare floorboards. He took a bag of Bonbons from his pocket and popped one in his mouth then offered the bag to Jim.

'No ta, lad. I keep tellin' you, toffee in't on the menu when you got teeth like mine. And your bike'll come a lot quicker if you cut back on 'em 'n all.'

'I know but I can't help it...I just can't stop. It's like a disease.'

'Maybe so but you'll end up with teeth like mine if y' aren't careful.'

Toby put the sweets away as Jim brought over two mugs of steaming tea. He placed one on the old pine table beside Toby and the other he cupped firmly in his leathery old hands. He sat in the chair beside his young friend and they stared at the glowing coals through the open door of the Rayburn. The coals shifted in the grate and a spray of sparks went up the flu.

'Are you looking forward to Christmas?' asked Toby, dreamily.

'Oh, Christmas is a time for you young 'uns,' replied Jim, 'not us ol' folk. I expect you are though. Going anywhere?'

'No. Grandma and Grandpa are coming down Christmas Day. Are you going anywhere?'

'Na…I'll…be 'ere,' said Jim, coughing halfway through his reply.

'Do you have anyone coming?' asked Toby, blowing a succession of quick gentle puffs into his mug.

'No, now Nerys has passed, it'll just be me.' Jim reached for his lighter and relit his stubby cigarette.

'Don't you have any children…or grandchildren?'

The old man cackled and then wheezed and then coughed. 'You have to 'ave been married for that lad…somethin' I never got round to doing.'

'Why not?' Toby asked sipping his tea.

'Guess I jus' never did. Nerys…well her 'usband died young n' from then on it always seemed to be jus' the two of us.'

'Miss her badly, don't you?' It was a statement more than a question and Toby didn't expect an answer. He put down his mug and reached for another Bonbon.

'Place in't the same without her,' said Jim, finding memories in the coals. 'Not sure I like it now.'

'If I ask mum and she says it's okay would you like to come and spend Christmas with us?'

The old man's brow lifted.

'Oh, I don't think yer mother needs another mouth to feed. She's got enough on 'er plate already.'

'Go on, it'll be fun. We can play charades and stuff,' said Toby.

'I dunno what that is, but thanks lad. But like I said, Christmas is a time for family.'

'But what if you don't have one? Think about it. I'll ask anyway,' said Toby sipping his tea again. 'You can't spend Christmas on your own!'

A short while later after Toby had finished his tea he wrapped himself up again to go home.

'Well, don't forget nex' Friday lad,' said Jim, as Toby stepped out into the crisp chill evening. 'You'll get ya Christmas box.'

The following week went by in an ever-increasing blur of festive anticipation and on the last day of school, Toby's excitement had reached a new high. Although no more snow fell, the weather remained clear and cold. Toby's mum had been surprised when he had asked if ol' Jim could spend Christmas Day with them and had initially refused but when he asked her for the fourth day running, she was impressed with his compassion and began to have second thoughts. Ralph wasn't happy about the idea at all.

'Why you want to have that old man here anyway? I'll tell you one thing, if he does come, he ain't sitting next to me!'

'Good cos' he wouldn't want to,' answered Toby defiantly. 'And anyway he can sit next to me. I'm the one who wants him here. How would you like to spend Christmas Day all by yourself?'

'If it meant not seeing you, yeah I wouldn't mind.'

'Now now, you two,' interposed their mother. 'Ralph, have a little compassion for an old man who's just lost his only family and Toby, you can tell Mr Worthingshaw he's welcome to join us.'

'Great, thanks mum,' said Toby, sticking his tongue out at Ralph. Getting one over on his brother was always satisfying but it often meant dodging an incoming slap. 'What time can he come?'

'He ain't sitting next to me,' snarled Ralph.

'Oh, I don't know. Around noon? Perhaps he'd like a sherry first.'

'I'll go tell him,' said Toby, running to the coat hook in the hall.

'Oh no you won't, young man,' his mother called out after him, 'it's bedtime. You can tell him tomorrow... after we've been to Mayford.'

And with a grin that almost connected his ears, Toby went upstairs to brush his teeth.

Dawn came up bright and frosty. After breakfast Toby went with his mother to town to help with her last minute shopping. They traipsed around the bustling supermarket for fresh groceries and a suitably sized turkey, then up Mayford's steep high street to the butcher's for some sausages. Then it was time for Toby to do his own shopping. In the market he found a brush and comb set etched with an oriental flower design for his mother to replace the brush whose handle she had broken months ago but repaired with tape. She would tut and complain every morning when using it, telling herself that she really must get a new one but she never did. For Ralph, he bought a small box of fishing tackle, complete with two reels of line and an assortment of floats and weights. With fishing being his big brother's newest hobby, Toby's mother had confided that she had bought Ralph a new rod and thought that some new tackle would compliment it perfectly. For his grandpa, he bought a small tube of toffees and for his grandma some of her favourite vanilla fudge. Finally and with a little help from his mother, some whiskey chocolates for ol' Jim.

As the afternoon wore on the sky clouded over and it became increasingly cold and gloomy. But the decorations and lights that brightened every shop window and adorned each lamppost imbued the town with a warmth that seemed to counter the weather. In the square outside the chemist, several members of the choir from St. Matthew's huddled together in a close semi-circle and sang carols. Scurrying passers-by would stop awhile and become appreciative onlookers for a few minutes, all glowing cheeks and sparkling eyes, until the cold began to nip at their feet and coerce them to continue their hurried business.

After devouring well-deserved cups of tea and currant buns in the station café, Toby and his mother clambered aboard the four o'clock bus. They collapsed exhausted onto a seat with shopping bags all around them. Toby wasn't looking forward to trudging out on his paper-round when he got home – but then again, it was the Friday before Christmas and the evening he was due to collect the many promises of 'a little something extra', so his fatigue was somewhat diluted by that fact. Plus he was looking forward to informing Jim that he wouldn't have to spend Christmas alone. So, when a little over two hours later - having wolfed down bangers and mash - Toby set off on his round, nobody would have guessed from his energy and enthusiasm that he had been on his feet all day.

A bitter north-easterly whipped up after sunset and brought with it a snowflake or two. The temperature hovered around zero but Toby was oblivious to it. He was glowing from the warmth of human kindness that was being shown him by his customers. At almost every door he knocked on he received a hearty 'thank you' and a treat of some kind – be it a larger than usual tip or some sweets. The Browns - usually so frugal - surprised Toby the most by giving him five pounds plus a box of Santa shaped chocolates. Most others paid for their papers with a pound note and told him to keep the change and a few even gave him a pound on top of that. The slog back up Hillside View was much harder than usual because Mr and Mrs Marmaduke had presented him with a big jar of Humbugs; so even though the sack was light on papers, it was heavy on booty.

Overjoyed at his good fortune and full of expectation for his final two calls, Toby made the long trudge down Weir Farm Lane to Douglas's Mill. The wind rattled the bare branches of the ancient oaks that towered either side of him and every now and then a strong gust would rush up behind him and send him forward on his toes. He pictured himself riding a shiny new bike and thought that maybe next month when he saw Colonel Douglas, the white moustachioed war hero wouldn't complain about the lateness of the delivery because Toby could go back to doing his round before tea. Like Mrs Ashcroft, Colonel Douglas was a person of habit and apparently enjoyed reading his evening paper over an aperitif before dinner. However, since Toby had been burdened with doing his round on foot, the stern gentleman had been forced to peruse the Echo whilst sipping his after dinner port in his wing-backed chair beside the fireplace.

It wasn't totally unexpected, but Toby received nothing more than the usual sixty pence from the Colonel who greeted him at the front door with a gruff - 'How do you do?' And all he got by way of a seasonal good wish was - 'Enjoy your two days off.' As if to make amends for her uncharitable husband, Mrs Douglas, a sweet natured, timid woman who always dressed as if she was going somewhere posh met Toby at the gate in the red brick garden wall as he started back up the lane. With a conspiratorial glance over her shoulders, she presented him with a tin of shortbread biscuits she had baked that afternoon. For a few seconds Toby was lost for words.

'You're welcome, my dear,' she said, noticing his surprise. 'And have a very happy Christmas.' Her smile was so warm and genuine that Toby felt as though she had embraced him.

He put the tin in his sack along with the Humbugs and other goodies and even though just one paper remained inside, the sack bulged with the spoils he had collected. Its weight, as it bumped heavily against his hip with every step, felt very satisfying indeed.

When he finally knocked on ol' Jim's door, Toby's excitement was fluttering in his stomach like tickets in a Tombola drum.

'Come in lad, come in,' coughed Jim. 'Is it snowin' yet? Radio says we're likely t'get some more.'

'A few flurries,' replied Toby, handing Jim his paper, 'but nothing much. It's flippin' cold though.'

'That'll be the wind. Come in and warm y'self.'

Toby entered the kitchen and set his jacket and scarf over the back of a chair. His face and hands tingled as an immediate thaw set in and he sat down and stretched his feet towards the Rayburn.

'Fancy a chessnut?' said Jim, pointing to a wooden bowl on the table. 'Freshly roasted.'

'Is that what I can smell?' asked Toby, sniffing the air.

'Good 'int it? Go on, try one.'

Toby took one of the charred nuts and, following Jim's example, dug his thumbnail in and pulled it apart. It tasted powdery and nasty and he puckered his face.

'Don't like it, eh? Good. More f'me,' said Jim, filling the teapot.

'Guess what I got,' said Toby, emptying his sack onto the table.

'Blimey, who's the lucky one then?'

Toby opened the biscuit tin and inhaled the burnt butter smell of the golden biscuits.

'Corr! These smell good. Let's have one with our cuppa?'

'Sounds good to me, lad,' said Jim, flicking his cigarette into the open oven and then pouring the tea.

'Oh, Mum said it's okay for you to come for Christmas lunch.'

'She did now?' Jim eyed his young friend suspiciously.

'Uh huh. She said you can come for a sherry around twelve, if you want.'

'That's awful nice but with your grandparents comin' n' all...'

The old man wasn't used to getting social invitations and had dismissed it from his mind soon after Toby had first mentioned it. He had suspected that the boy was only being polite and wouldn't really ask his mother but now, he felt uneasy at the prospect of being an outsider in a family's get-together and wanted to find an excuse to decline. However he didn't get the chance because Toby interrupted him insisting that if a person had no family to spend Christmas with, then surely the next best thing was to spend it with friends.

'...and we're friends, aren't we?'

'Course we are, lad...but...'

'Then that's settled,' said Toby, drawing the discussion to an end.

Jim was resigned but a little surprised too. He handed Toby his mug of tea and as he took one of the shortbreads that was offered, he patted Toby's shoulder.

'Okay lad, you win. 'N thanks.' A brief smile stretched his cracked lips as he tried to remember the last time he sat down to a well-prepared meal, least of all a Christmas lunch. Neither him, nor Nerys had bothered much when it came to such things.

They both sat munching while reviewing the gifts that were spread over the table. Toby was grateful for everything.

'Oh yeah. And I reckon I got nearly twenty pounds to put towards my bike.'

'All of it?' laughed Jim into his tea mug. 'You mean...you won't spend any of it on them toffees ya so fond of?'

'Don't need to,' said Toby, clasping the jar of brown and white Humbugs, 'not for a while anyway. And I'm bound to get more sweets for Christmas.'

'Are ya now?' said Jim, getting up. He walked towards the cluttered pine dresser and picked something up. 'Which reminds me…'

'Here we go,' thought Toby, 'here it comes. The big one.' He tried to appear blasé about it by reading the label on the jar of Humbugs as if his Christmas box wasn't that important but he was so excited he couldn't even focus on the words.

'Here ya go lad. There's a little extra for you in there too.' Toby reached out and took the coins that were offered.

'Thanks Jim…you shouldn't of.'

The old man made a sound as if to say, 'oh be quiet, it's nothing,' and sat back down with his tea. Toby counted the money. One pound exactly - sixty pence for the papers and forty pence for himself.

'Forty pence?' he thought. 'Is that all? Is that what you've been harping on about for the last two months?' His disappointment was crushing and filled his mouth with a bitterness that he couldn't swallow and for a few moments Toby was speechless. After all, this was the bonus that would enable him to get the Road Warrior 5000. He wasn't sure whether to laugh out loud at his unrealistic expectations or to cry in despair at the thought of having to do his paper-round on foot for months and months to come.

Jim coughed again, convulsing forwards and trembling with the effort as a string of saliva dribbled from his mouth onto the floor. Toby moved to offer a pat on the back but stopped and for the first time, saw an old man whose trousers no longer fit him and had to be gathered at the waist and whose socks were full of holes. It suddenly occurred to him just how poorly Jim lived and involuntarily he glanced around the small, nicotine and soot stained kitchen with a critical eye. As warm as it was, it was also gloomy and cluttered and in desperate need of painting. Smoke stained wallpaper had long ago peeled away from the top of the walls, dried into brittle curls by the heat from the Rayburn. Beneath the window beside the back door was a bench that looked like it belonged in a church and folded untidily at one end of it were several blankets. Knowing how cold and dark the rest of the cottage was, Toby could well imagine the old man settling down on its hard unforgiving surface for the night just to be in a room with some warmth.

Just then, forty pence didn't seem such a trivial amount and Toby realised that even though others had given more, everyone had given what they could afford. More important perhaps was that they had wanted to give anything at all.

'Every little helps Jim,' he said, thinking of Ryan's words. 'I'll put it with the rest. And thanks again.'

'You're a good lad,' said Jim, wiping the back of a hand across his mouth. 'Aren't many your age would bother cheering up an old man.'

They finished their tea in silence and then a short while later, Toby gathered his things, put on his coat and scarf and made his way to the door.

'I'll come and get you just before twelve on Christmas Day then,' he said, putting on his gloves and lifting the strap of the sack over his shoulder.

'I'll be ready,' said Jim, patting Toby's back. 'Perhaps I'll even dig out me Sunday best,' he added with a chuckle that turned into a wheeze.

When Toby got home, he told his mother that Jim had accepted the invitation and that he would go and collect him just before midday. Then, he sat down on the floor by the fireside and showed her all of his gifts and whilst his mother made him a mug of hot chocolate, he counted up his money. When she returned with his drink, she helped herself to one of his biscuits.

'Mmm, not bad. Fancy sneaking out to the side gate just to give you these,' said Toby's mother with an accusing air. 'Afraid of him, she is…him and military ways. Still thinks he's in the army, I reckon.'

A little later when Toby's mother turned off his bedroom light, he closed his eyes and instantly fell asleep.

A dull, overcast Christmas Eve came and went in a frenzy of preparation for the following day. In between watching Bedknobs and Broomsticks and getting halfway through a thousand-piece jigsaw puzzle of the characters from The Jungle Book, Toby helped his mother peel potatoes and make a trifle. After tea when the curtains were drawn and the flames licked gently at the coals in the hearth, the Monopoly board came out but when Toby and Ralph started fighting over first dibs on the re-mortgaged Mayfair and Park Lane their mother decided to call time on the wheeling and dealing. The three of them then sat down with mugs of hot chocolate and watched television but it wasn't long before Toby took himself off to bed. He wanted to fall asleep as quickly as possible in order to hurry in the morning. However, such was his excitement that he laid awake tossing and turning until close to midnight.

Eventually though, sleep came to him and before he knew it, he was walking up the road towards Number Two, The Street having unwrapped all his presents that had mysteriously appeared around the base of the Christmas tree during the night. He didn't get the Grand Prix racing set he had wanted or any money to put towards his new bike but the battery operated racing car and a few other odds and ends and sweets that he did receive made it fairly easy to hide his disappointment. His mother was delighted with her hairbrush and comb set and thought the oriental flower pattern was very pretty. Ralph punched him on the arm in appreciation of his fishing tackle.

'Nice one kiddo,' he said.

But once the presents were opened Toby was eager for midday to arrive. His grandparents were due around the same time - bringing with them another present or two - and as he walked through the village to collect ol' Jim, he kept a lookout for their car. The day was overcast but bright, not dull and gloomy like the day before and the church bells rang out merrily.

Toby knocked on Jim's door just before twelve o'clock. Across the low privet hedge, the door to number one opened and a longhaired young man carrying a motorcycle helmet emerged. He wore a black leather jacket and sturdy black leather boots. He stood on the doorstep and, taking the raw morning air deep into his lungs, he exhaled and watched his plume of steam rise upwards and disappear into the white sky.

'Won't be long,' he said to someone inside as he pulled the door closed. Then noticing Toby standing next door he said - 'You'll be waiting there a long time, boy. The old man's gone.'

Toby looked back along the street and said, 'But I would've passed him.' The young man mumbled something impatiently and opened his front door again.

'Mum,' he called. 'Mum!' He disappeared inside and re-emerged a few seconds later with his mother, whom Toby recognised as Mrs Hopkins from the Post Office. She was a robust woman with thick curly brown hair and she wore a large flowery pinafore tied around her substantial middle.

'Oh dear,' she exclaimed on seeing Toby. The longhaired young man opened the adjoining garage door, put on his helmet and disappeared inside. His mother waddled around the hedge to where Toby was standing.

'You probably haven't heard, have you dear?' she said in a caring but slightly impatient manner.

'Heard what?' asked Toby, shaking his head slowly from side to side. She put an arm around his shoulders and drew him away from Jim's door towards her own. A motorbike suddenly blasted into life shattering the morning peace, it's exhaust echoing loudly in the garage and then the young man in the black leathers emerged on it and sped off up the road. When the roar of the engine faded, Mrs Hopkins continued.

'He spoke very highly of you, you know. Such a nice young man, he said. In fact his last thoughts were of you and he left me something to give you.'

'What do you mean?' asked Toby still not understanding what could have made ol' Jim want to miss his Christmas lunch.

Mrs Hopkins turned and looked down into Toby's puzzled face.

'Poor ol' Jim passed away yesterday afternoon.'

For Toby, Christmas turned out to be full of conflicting emotions. An unpleasant but familiar sense of loss followed him home, as did the envelope that Mrs Hopkins had given him. In it was a card from Jim in which he had scribbled – A little sumthin your mother and me thawt of. Hope you'll still drop in for tea. There was nothing else in the card to hint at what he and his mother had thought of and so it made no sense and as Toby tried to understand what the words meant, his tears smudged the ink. At home, his grandparents were sympathetic with kind words and comforting hugs, his mother less so saying - 'It's a part of life to lose those we're fond of. We just have to accept it. You'll be all right in a day or two. Now be a good boy and come and help me in the kitchen.'

When Toby passed Jim's cottage a couple of days later, his stomach tightened and a lump rose in his throat but he was no longer tearful. He had dealt with loss before and possibly owing to his mother's insistence that he not be weepy, his handling of bereavement belied his years. For certain, he felt sad but it was a sadness for the hole in his own life rather than a sadness for his friend because he believed that Jim had been reunited with Nerys, possibly the only grown up he had ever loved and for that, Toby was glad. He would miss his evening visits to Number Two, sitting in front of the Rayburn with a mug of tea talking about this and that and he would never forget the things he'd learned from his wise old friend. He was sure that one day when he was growing his own runner beans or looking to snare a rabbit, all the knowledge that Jim had shared would come in handy. For the time being though, he would remember this

Christmas as the one ol' Jim helped get him the best present ever for when he had followed his mother into the kitchen, waiting for him was a Road Warrior 5000 with the three speed twisting hand grip and side-stand.

He pedalled off down Weir Farm Lane whooping and hollering gleefully into the wind as it whistled past his ears. It felt amazing to be on two wheels again. Maybe Colonel Douglas would be a little happier now that he was going to get his paper delivered before dinner.

Stepping Stones

A black Range Rover slips out of the car park on Rochester Row and accelerates towards the lights where it joins a queue of cars waiting to turn left onto Vauxhall Bridge Road. It is 18:27 on this particular Thursday and London is still in the grip of its evening rush hour.

Behind the wheel sits Robert Cornelius Wickham – owner of Wickham Construction Ltd in Amberton, Kent. Robert has just come from a meeting with an old university chum and his excitement at its earlier than expected outcome is plain to see. He is sporting the broadest of grins on his chubby forty-two year old face and he congratulates himself repeatedly as though he has just found a breakthrough cure for cancer. Yes, anyone seeing him drive past will think, there goes a very happy man.

Robert thumbs a button on the steering wheel and Luciano Pavarotti's towering tenor sweeps away the silence in the Range Rover's cabin like a tsunami assaulting a quiet seaside town. He then fiddles with the heating controls for it is cold outside and on his walk back to the car he had to endure a piercing north easterly wind. Robert knows he will not be home for at least two hours but the thought does little to wipe the smile from his face.

The lights are a long time red and so he calls home to let Patricia, his wife, know he will be back early.

La Boheme becomes a background whisper as the Bluetooth connects and a dialling tone issues from the car's eight speakers. Patricia does not answer but a voicemail recording does. Robert's grin falters briefly as he leaves a short message. No "Honey", no "Darling", no "Sweetheart" – just the simple fact that he will be home a couple of hours earlier than he thought. Sweet sentiment was just one of the things that had deserted their union a while ago. Financial indifference together with Robert's self-absorbed focus to make a success of his business had long ago soured his wife's opinion of him. As far as she was concerned, he was to blame for their all too ordinary lifestyle and its complete lack of glamour. In their early days together he had promised her the world and she had believed him but it was a promise that he had not kept.

Of course, Robert knows why she had not answered, or at least he has a strong suspicion. He is quite sure she is having an affair and that she is no doubt making the most of his absence at this very moment. The distasteful thought forces an image into his mind of another man in his bed servicing his wife and a mask of concrete draws itself quickly across his face. Concern mixed with embarrassment pulls his lips into a thin tight line. With whom she was carrying on he knows not nor does he want to; he just hopes that it is merely a fling and that she avoids doing anything rash. At least until all the contracts are signed and work has begun on the deal he has just made. Then she will be come back to him. However, unfortunately for Robert, without his wife's signature, the deal simply will not happen.

The lights change and the line of cars moves forward until Robert finds himself at the front facing another red. Two waves of pedestrians step off the kerbs left and right and meet in the middle of the road like curtains drawn across a window only to be re-opened immediately as each wave continues crossing to the other side. Red buses inch forward beyond them, their engines rallying to a citywide diesel soundtrack, their seats filled with uninterested, weary faces. Robert loosens his tie, lowers his window an inch and lights a cigar. Smoke curls out the gap to join the cocktail of London's other pollutants. He feels glad that he does not have to endure this everyday and his smile returns.

Robert often finds solace in his belief in destiny. He holds firm a belief that people's lives are peppered with life-shaping events and that each event is a stepping-stone of opportunity to something better or to something worse. It is not always easy to identify the profitable steps from the fruitless but wisdom is a useful ally in recognising which is which and if one chooses wisely and without fear, particularly when a choice might seem difficult to make or even morally dubious, then he believes that one cannot fail but to attain one's fortune. There is no doubt whatsoever in his mind that destiny was responsible for his afternoon's triumph.

The lights change to green. Robert turns left between two more waiting waves of pedestrians and joins the slow moving traffic crossing the Thames. He passes the MI6 building and soon after, the Oval cricket ground on his way home.

Home is a former farm just outside the village of Brook in the heart of the Kent countryside. Brook is a pretty little place, particularly when the sun shines but it suffers from a common scourge of the modern world - an excess of traffic. Its situation is such that it is a convenient cut-through from the nearby town of Amberton to the main artery that links London to the Kent coast and the port of Dover. The narrow road that serves as the village's main thoroughfare is often in poor condition with potholes appearing as fast as they are filled and soft verges frequently collapsing under the sheer weight of passing vehicles. Several of the roadside cottages have had to be repaired owing to the constant vibrations from cars and lorries, garden walls have sustained damage and cats have been run over. Signed petitions to the local council for a by-pass have for years been either ignored or turned down on the grounds of expense and interim measures such as sleeping policemen have done little to curb the problem. However, a turning point came late last year when old Jack Humphries, a resident of Brook for over half a century, was killed by a speeding car as he cycled back from the little off-licence at Amberton where the poor fellow had gone to pick up a bottle of his favourite malt whiskey. Unfortunately, the off-licence is located on a blind corner on the way out of Amberton and it has been the site of frequent incidents. Within a month of renewed protests and local newspaper coverage, the by-pass had been given the green light by the council.

The traffic going into Brixton is bumper to bumper and it gives Robert the chance to try Patricia again. This time he rings her mobile more from wanting to disrupt the tryst she is likely enjoying than to speak to her. But she still does not answer and Robert does not leave a message. He wonders if there is any hope for their marriage. He hopes so.

The series of stepping-stones that led to his afternoon meeting started years ago when Robert was a young man in university. During his first year, the death of a fellow student brought him, for the first time in his life, face to face with the ugly side of human nature. The student, Dylan Evans, a socially awkward and gangly Glaswegian in his final year of study, had one day got involved in a blazing row with one of his roommates. He then proceeded to get very drunk. A meteor display had been predicted for that night and Dylan had unwisely decided to crawl out of a skylight window to watch the spectacle from the flat roof above the dormitories. At some point in his inebriated state, he had got up onto the parapet, slipped and fallen to his death. The resulting inquest ruled accidental death by broken neck. But Robert knew there was more to it than that.

Robert had already been out on the roof watching the night sky when Dylan appeared. Not wanting to be discovered by the senior student (the roof was out of bounds to all), Robert had hidden behind a nearby chimney stack. He was relieved when Dylan quickly fell into an alcohol-induced sleep and was just about to return inside when he saw two more students crawl out the skylight. They found Dylan snoring and joked about giving him the fright of his life by waking him while pretending to throw him over the parapet. Robert watched as they picked Dylan up and made to hurl him over the edge like they would a rolled up old carpet into a waiting skip below all the while taunting him to wake up. Unfortunately, one of them lost their grip on Dylan's ankles as they swung out wide and

Dylan went over. The other student, unable to manage the weight and momentum of the body on his own, could not prevent Dylan from going all the way.

While it might have been a practical joke that went horribly wrong, the two students were certainly to blame for Dylan's death. And Robert had seen who those two students were. He had seen their faces in the moonlight as clearly as if he had shone a torch at them. Luckily for him, the two horrified students quickly disappeared inside without knowing Robert was watching. What they might have done if they had found him there caused him much discomfort.

It was several hours before Robert found the courage to go back in because fear had frozen him to the spot. Fear had also prevented him from telling anyone what he had seen, fear of retaliation, of being expelled, of even being considered an accessory and so, with no evidence to the contrary, the two students, Drew Whitby and Alistair Nash got away with Dylan's death.

The Range Rover continues its journey southwards out of London, a single life-carrying cell among thousands of others squeezing through the city's network of veins. Its progress is painfully slow as it heads up over the ridge of Crystal Palace, where two television transmitters stand like giant sentinels gazing out over a domain that covers vast swathes of London and the Home Counties.

Robert overcomes the tedium with thoughts of the future. As soon as Patricia has signed the land over to him for development and his application from the council has been approved, he can start building his vision and their future. Once she sees how much money it will bring in, she will quit fooling around behind his back and be the wife he always hoped she would be. They can take a nice long holiday, maybe travel the world and make a fresh start. Perhaps even a second honeymoon. So much to look forward to.

The university incident affected the young Robert deeply and his studies and grades suffered as a result. He had blamed himself for not having prevented the tragedy and again for not having the courage to admit to the police what he had witnessed. In a way, he had considered himself a third party to the crime for assisting Whitby and Nash with his silence and for several months he had been plagued with nightmares. Throughout this time, he became morose and unsociable and completely lost his appetite which consequently made him ill until eventually, he had to drop out of university altogether. Fortunately for Robert, time is a merciful healer and the memories of that night gradually abated until one day he thought of Nash and Whitby no more.

Then one evening five weeks ago, Robert happened to be watching the nine o'clock news when a ghost from his past appeared on the screen. Alistair Nash had just been appointed to government. Robert had immediately recognised the student in the man on camera and in a moment of suffocating regression, all the horror of that night came rushing back. For several minutes he was speechless. Immobilised. That night in bed, he tossed and turned and floundered in sickening recollections about that starry evening back in university, about the effect it had on him and his life and about the two killers who should have seen justice. Then as the dawn light broke and the silent shadows across the countryside became real living things his mind began to clear and he suddenly realised that he was facing an opportunity. He realised that nothing could change the past, what was done was done and yet plenty could change the future. The fact that Alistair Nash had just joined the Department for Communities and Local Government was all the proof Robert needed to believe that once again, destiny had shown him a stepping-stone.

His meeting with Nash had gone better than he thought for in truth Robert had been quite nervous heading into it. He had no idea how Nash would react. However, he need not have worried because the Rt. Hon "gentleman" cracked like a walnut tempting fate on a dance floor. It was obvious that Nash had been living with the incident never far from his thoughts because as soon as Robert had stated his intention, Nash had offered anything that was in his power in exchange for Robert's continued silence.

Of course, Nash hadn't known whether Robert was bluffing, if he really had seen anything on the rooftop that night. He didn't even know if anyone would believe the story after so many years but it was clearly a risk too big to take for someone on his way up the political ladder. At the very least it would create a scandal and force him to resign. The case may even be reopened and despite the lack of physical evidence, there was Whitby and now Wickham who could testify against him. No, Nash thought the smartest thing to do was to play along, to do whatever Robert asked and in the meantime figure out the best course of action. There had to be some way of burying this permanently. He had worked too damn hard and waited too damn long to get into the hallowed halls of Parliament and he wasn't going to give it all up over a tragic accident that happened years ago.

What Robert asked of him was simple. The Amberton-Brook Bypass as it was now officially known, had two possible planned routes. The favourite of locals and councillors was one that went through a large part of Robert's land, although legally it was Patricia's land bequeathed her by her parents along with the farm. Robert still had to persuade her to sign the land over to him but he considered that a minor hurdle in comparison to influencing the council's decision. His reasoning was that any compensation for the land from the government would be peanuts compared to what he could make if he used the land for housing, especially if he built and sold the houses himself.

At their meeting, arranged by Robert to take place in the neutral surrounds of the bar in St. Ermins Hotel, close to St. James's Park, Nash was told that in return for his silence Robert demanded that the bypass be constructed along the alternative route, no matter how much opposition the decision would create among the local community. He also demanded assurance that his planning application for a small housing development on the land (which Robert had shown him a copy of) was given swift and unobstructed approval. Robert had stated with a confidence he had not fully felt, that he considered what he was asking to be of no significant difficulty for a man in Nash's position. Nash had agreed to do all he could but admitted that he could make no promises. As Robert had risen to leave at the end of the meeting, he had revealed a strategically pinned microphone, declaring it to be his insurance. He had walked away leaving Nash looking like a condemned man. The microphone was just a ruse but it had had the desired affect.

It isn't until Robert passes through Orpington that he finally puts the pervading orange hue of urban streetscapes behind him. At last he feels free of the capital's suffocating grip. It has been a little over two hours since he pulled out of the car park in SW1 and it is the first time tonight that the Range Rover's headlights are actually lighting the way. Back in familiar territory with the dark countryside surrounding him like a hooded cloak it is also the first time that he senses his conscience biting its lip. Blackmail is a dirty word not to mention a criminal act and although he had considered this carefully all the time he was planning his little scheme it is only now as he drives along a lonely country road that he wonders what he might do if Alistair Nash decides to not play ball, that he does not want to live with his lie any longer, to come clean. Would the deal simply be called off with no harm done or would Nash seek an investigation into Robert's attempt at extortion?

Robert had been mindful of the possibility of Nash confessing to his part in Evans's killing rather than allowing himself to be blackmailed and he knew if that happened, it would place him up on that roof too. For how else would he know about it? And if he had been up there, why had he not come forward at the time and admitted what he had seen? Perhaps, they might say, he was a third pair of hands that had thrown Evans to the ground. Robert had considered these scenarios and questions as well as countless others over the last few weeks but he had always managed to assuage himself that he could simply plead ignorance in any investigation, that he had absolutely no idea Nash was anywhere near that roof. It had simply been a bad joke he had dreamt up and played on an old friend. How was he to know there was any truth in it? In the end, it would come down to Robert's word against Nash's. A politician with an admission of guilt to a killing or an upstanding local businessman with not a blemish on his record – not even a parking ticket.

The Pavarotti CD had finished some time ago but Robert has been so engrossed in his thoughts that he has not noticed. Now, in the quiet cabin of the Range Rover, he breathes a sigh of relief as his safety net of an ignorance plea soothes his fears. Those fears had made him tense and he notices how rigid his body is, white knuckles gripping the steering wheel, shoulders and neck, arms and legs fixed as though in rigor mortis. Another deep lungful of cool, recycled air bleeds the anxiety from his body like pressure escaping from a tyre. He tells himself for the umpteenth time that he has absolutely nothing to worry about and absolutely nothing to lose.

But a great deal to gain.

In a couple of years when his vision has come to pass, when the houses are built and sold off, he considers it not unreasonable to expect a two or three million pound profit.

Yes, today he definitely struck out onto a profitable stepping-stone.

The Range Rover continues navigating the dark roads of Kent. Other vehicles come and go, headlights dazzling, taillights blushing, but compared to a short while ago, Robert is travelling in a virtually deserted nightscape. He passes a signpost that includes

Amberton and his excitement returns full strength. For the first time in a long time he is actually looking forward to seeing Patricia, to revealing his plans to her, to seeing the look on her face when she learns what they will soon be worth. Of course, he will omit the part about blackmailing a politician and instead simply tell her that he knows someone in a high place who can help. He will then work on persuading her to sign the land over to his company for development. She has long held ideas of her own for the land but as Robert has often told her, an animal sanctuary will bring them little more than hardship and foul smells.

His phone rings and he sees Patricia's name displayed. Before he has even uttered a greeting she is asking where he is and how is it that his meeting ended so soon and why did he not call to let her know he would be home early. She sounds flustered, irritated. Robert is not surprised but he is annoyed that his wife takes him for such a fool. He resists the temptation to argue with her and instead asks where she has been.

'I'm at home,' she replies.

He feigns surprise and queries why she had not answered the phone when he called earlier. Where has she been and what has she been doing? She mumbles something about having probably just missed his call as she had popped out to the supermarket in Amberton around that time. In fact, she is still there. Despite believing it to be a lie (who spends two hours at the supermarket?) Robert asks her to pick up a bottle of Champagne while she is there and explains that when he gets home, he has some news that will warrant a little celebration. Patricia sounds surprised, curious and says she is heading to that aisle now. She hangs up without so much as a goodbye.

For the second time today, Robert cannot conceal his excitement. The fact that Patricia was flustered proves that she still has feelings for him. She has not completely given up on their marriage or surely she would not care about hurting him. He applies a little more pressure to the pedal under his right foot and the Range Rover picks up speed. Another signpost states that Amberton is eight miles away.

Of course, Patricia is not at the supermarket in Amberton, nor has she been near a supermarket all day. She had met her lover, local radio celebrity Roger Styles, for brunch in Sevenoaks after which, the couple had spent the entire afternoon at his home near Tonbridge making love. Taking it for granted that her work-obsessed husband was away in London and was likely to be back later than he suggested rather than earlier, she had left her phone in her car. It was only now as she got in to drive home that she saw his missed call. And panicked.

She panicked because she knows she has to get home before Robert in order to make it appear she has been there. She had left this morning before the milkman came so there will be two bottles still sitting outside and the post will be on the doormat. Two sure signs that nobody has been home all day. Her marriage is over, of that she is quite certain but this is not the time for Robert to discover she has been seeing someone else. Besides, at the moment she is just rediscovering her womanhood and having fun. She knows in her heart that she could never get seriously involved with a man like Roger. Beneath his charming and exciting exterior, he is insincere and, she suspects, nothing more than a vain gigolo.

She quickly calculates the time it will take her to drive to Amberton, to pick up a bottle of Champagne from the supermarket and then get back home. She realises it is going to be a close call and she considers leaving out the Champagne altogether. Perhaps she could fob her husband off by saying the supermarket had sold out but the poor excuse brings a frown to her handsome face. She pushes the gearlever forward and guns her little Mazda away from Roger's love nest.

As usual, if it were not for the two pubs and three fast food outlets in the high street, Amberton at 9pm would be asleep. The supermarket at the southern edge of town stays awake for an hour beyond that but by midnight, the town is dormant. The Range Rover murmurs gently past a man eating a kebab as he sits on the bench outside the Post Office and then a group of smokers huddling together on the pavement outside the Maidens Head. Halfway along the high street Robert turns left and takes the overused road to Brook. It is a fairly straight albeit uneven ribbon of tarmac and therefore quite easy to breach the speed limit but in the pitch dark of night, headlights give fair warning of any oncoming traffic and so Robert increases his speed. He knows this stretch of road probably better than any other, which is useful when your mind is on other things and his mind is filled with his impending happiness and of the possibility of a future with the woman he still loves. If only he could make her love him again.

He feathers the brake pedal before the bend by the off-licence and is about to get back on the throttle when a pale face suddenly appears in his high beams.

There is a loud bang and a sickening vibration that shudders through the cabin. Robert slams on the brakes and brings the big Range Rover to a stuttering halt. His heart lurches into his throat and all he can hear is it banging in his ears. He throws his gaze to the rear-view mirror as dread turns his stomach upside down. In the blood-red glow of his brake lights he sees a figure sprawled across the centre line of the road maybe thirty metres back, a dark unmoving shape, a pale hand here, a bare ankle there.

Robert is stunned.

A vacuum suddenly shrink-wraps itself around him and takes away his ability to breathe. He cannot hear and he cannot move. Seconds go by, each one seeming like a minute. His mind plays back the last thirty seconds as if an action replay would let him see something he missed.

BANG!

He panics and his breath comes rushing back in a desperate gasp to avoid suffocation. Then his hearing returns and the tinkle of a bell somewhere forces him to focus. He looks over his right shoulder and sees someone running out of the off-licence. Without really knowing why, Robert steps on the accelerator and tears off down the road towards Brook. His heartbeat is wild, his thoughts in turmoil.

Had he been paying more attention, had he been focussed on the road instead of dwelling on the joyful images his mind was creating, he might have noticed a familiar little Mazda parked on the verge opposite the off-licence.

Yes, stepping-stones. Some lead to something better, others to something worse.

Greetings from Saint Christopher

A gentle wind rattles the fronds of the palm trees and brings with it the pungent aroma of fiery Caribbean spices infused with sweet tropical fruits. Today's lunch – mango marinated Jerk Pork, rice 'n peas and as much salad as you like.

The grill chef continues ministering to the great slab of meat on the barbeque not twenty feet away and puffs of smoke rise from the griddle as fat sizzles onto the coals. The temptation to go and ask him for a pre-lunch sample is hard to resist but then, lunch is probably an hour or more away and the meat might not be ready. I tell myself that all good things are worth waiting for so I stay put and close my eyes. With indescribable satisfaction, I breathe in the aromatic cocktail of roasting meat, sea air and hot sand as my hammock sways gently in the breeze.

It seems only moments ago that I had whisked Naomi away from the surprise party that I, with the help of a few friends had organised in our village hall. It was in celebration of our first anniversary and everything had gone like clockwork, right down to the DJ playing our song while a large pink balloon carrying our holiday tickets floated down from the rafters into her waiting hands. It had taken weeks to plan but be it luck or simply the result of good organisation it had gone off without a hitch. For me, the highlight had been the moment I clicked on the lights and the assembled gang, friends and relatives alike, had all yelled, "SURPRISE!" The startled confusion on Naomi's face that quickly morphed into absolute delight was all the proof we needed to realise that she had been completely oblivious to the frantic preparations and arrangements that had been taking place behind her back during the preceding weeks. It was a wonderful moment that I shall cherish for a long, long time.

Later, with the buffet in ruins, the toasts all made and the slow dances over, we had said our goodbyes. Our destination - a two-hour drive away - had been a deluxe suite at the airport hotel prior to a morning flight to this island paradise.

Weeks of searching for the perfect location in which to celebrate our first year together had finally uncovered this little piece of heaven. It's situated in a south-facing lagoon and therefore sheltered from the trade winds that sweep in from the Atlantic. It's also a wonderfully unspoilt resort nestled within a horseshoe of lush green mountains that echo with the chatter of blue-headed parrots and scarlet macaws. Various treks and paths wind their way up into the hills and beg to be explored on foot or astride a donkey. It really is the ideal location for a romantic getaway and with an indolent eye I glance down at the turquoise water of the bay and give myself a mental pat on the back.

Great choice!

And yet something niggles me, something I must do before I can fully unwind...

Casting my mind back to the party, I know that I should have accepted a lift or booked a taxi to the airport. It wasn't so much because of the two or three glasses of Champagne I had enjoyed throughout the evening but rather the fact that I had been so utterly exhausted from rushing around here and there, organising DJs and catering and decorations and generally making sure everyone and everything would be in the right place at the right time when I arrived with Naomi. As the evening had worn on, the previous days began to catch up with me and fatigue had almost overwhelmed me but stubbornness together with the determination to see my plans through to the very end forced me to keep going. I had even given the drive to the airport careful consideration and the CD player had been primed to play a montage of our favourite songs. Call me soppy but what can I say...I'm still in love with the girl I married!

A waiter wearing a dazzlingly white jacket bearing the hotel's red and gold insignia on the breast pocket brings me a tall frosty glass of rum punch. I thank him and take it from his silver salver. Ice cubes tinkle gently. I savour its fruity bite and rest the glass on my bare stomach.

Beside me, a hammock hangs empty between two adjacent trees. It looks like a giant string bag entangled on a washing line. I wonder how Naomi is enjoying her snorkelling lesson and I push my sunglasses up onto my head to squint out over the bay. A small group of people are frolicking by a sunbathing platform that is anchored over a shallow reef. Their bodies float on the water like logs, barely disturbing the surface but then, a sudden jerking movement is followed by backsides pointing momentarily skywards before the logs disappear beneath the surface with a flourish of splashing feet.

Perhaps Naomi would know what is bugging me, what it is I think I've forgotten to take care of; I'll ask her when she comes back. And yet, even as I take another sip of my punch, I feel an overwhelming conviction that whatever it is cannot wait that long.

I rack my brains for the answer knowing that it's probably something utterly trivial, which of course only adds to its annoyance. At the same time my hand searches for the key to our room in the pocket of my shorts. Its credit card shape tells me that I can strike one possibility off the list. My hammock jiggles nervously as I stretch sideways to check that my sandals and towel are still close by and that Naomi's things are where she left them beneath the other hammock. It's all there. We had decided not to bring the camera with us today and so… Damn! What is it I've forgotten?

I had felt so tired driving to the airport that I'd actually considered pulling off the motorway for a short rest but the sight of Naomi, who was already dozing peacefully in the passenger seat, persuaded me to carry on. Also, by the time I had come across a rest area, perhaps bought a coffee to refresh myself it would have almost been morning and therefore a complete waste of the hotel booking. So instead, I had lowered the window a fraction to let a flow of cool invigorating air into the car.

Isn't it funny how time can appear to condense? One minute you're at a party in your village hall and the next, you're halfway around the world, swinging in a hammock in the shade of a palm tree. There's no doubting the old proverb - time certainly does fly when you're having fun.

The hairs on my arms waft in the breeze like corn in a field and my skin smells of summer - that sweet-smelling combination of sunburn and coconut oil. I take a long drink and relish the sensation of it meandering down my insides, cooling my pipes.

A chorus of breathless laughter reaches me from across the lagoon and I see the honeymooning couple that had come over on the same flight messing about in a hotel paddleboat, their enjoyment pure and unbridled. It brings to mind my own honeymoon last year when times had been a little harder and I couldn't treat my new wife to the holiday I had wanted. Instead, an unfortunately rainy week in Torquay had been all I could afford. Despite the weather, it had still been enjoyable.

The smell from the barbeque is making my stomach grumble impatiently and I wonder when Naomi will be heading back for lunch. I search for her across the bay and see her climb out of the water onto the sunbathing platform. She takes off her snorkelling mask and gives me a happy wave. I wave back and smile proudly.

My God, she looks great out there!

What a lucky guy I am and yet...oh damn, this is ridiculous! What could possibly be so urgent for me to do here? I'm on holiday for goodness sake! I haven't forgotten to turn the oven off at home or anything silly like that; the car is safely stowed at the airport and the passports are locked away in the safe in our room. There is absolutely nothing to do so for the love of God, relax and enjoy this heavenly setting!

I take a deep breath and try once more to let my tensions melt away in the tropical heat. This is what I have been looking forward to for so long, so whatever is bothering me can wait until I get home. I make a big deal of exhaling slowly and forcing my muscles to relax. My body's mass seems to increase and stretch the hammock closer to the sandy floor.

The gentle wind rouses the palms overhead with a sound like heavy rain and at long last, my body becomes heavy with slumber. A smile of pure indulgence spreads across my face as the melodious glee of the newlyweds mingles with the gentle lapping and fizzing of the nearby surf.

Somewhere in the lagoon a motorboat is slicing a wake across the water, its powerful outboard buzzing like a distant chainsaw ripping through a tree trunk. Without opening my eyes, I imagine the water-skier or paraglider being towed across the bay, their height no doubt giving them a wonderful birds-eye view of the resort. Maybe I'll try it myself in the coming days. The boat's motor gets louder and louder and louder until I feel it must be nearly upon me and then suddenly I flinch, like when waking from a falling dream.

An intense light hits me, searing through my closed eyelids making everything red and then, all at once, I remember where I am. I'm still on my way to the airport. My body tenses and I gasp as though I've been resuscitated.

I open my eyes and a blinding white light is all I see.

There is no time to think and barely time to react but some instinct within me heaves the steering wheel to the left. We swerve across the asphalt towards the left hand side of the carriageway as a blaring horn fills my ears and sweeps past my open window. The screech of tyres awakens me like a slap in the face and with my heart pounding violently, I realise that I had fallen asleep at the wheel.

Breathing heavily and wiping glistening cold sweat from my brow, I take my foot off the accelerator and straighten the car's line. In the rear-view mirror I see the lights of a car growing smaller as the driver I nearly hit continues on. I mumble scathing curses to myself for almost causing an awful accident and apologise profusely to the driver who was no doubt cursing my very existence. Feeling utterly mortified I glance at Naomi.

She stirs; the tip of her tongue appears and moistens her lips, and her eyes, heavy and full of sleep, blink open. She smiles and reaches out to touch my arm, asking huskily if we are there yet and with the blood still pounding in my ears I whisper back that it's not much further. All of a sudden, with my heart heavy with guilt, I feel very awake, very sober and very lucky!

Mission Improbable

Nathan had rarely seen his mother so angry. She was slamming cupboard doors as she put away the groceries. She was yelling at the dog to get out of from under her feet. It was unlike her. He was surprised. Shocked.

'How could you have given my recipe away, you thoughtless, thoughtless boy? And to that dreadful harpy of all people! Why do you think people pay me good money to make their Christmas cakes? You stupid, stupid…' She didn't need to finish. Nathan got the general idea.

She had lost her temper with him before, that wasn't unusual. Like the time he had dropped her favourite crystal vase after being told not to play with it. Or when he had smacked a friend across the face for blowing out the candles on his eleventh birthday cake. But this was different. This was another level of anger entirely. The intensity that was swelling the veins in her neck and turning her face scarlet was something else. She looked ready to explode.

And Nathan's attempts to placate her seemed only to add to her rage. His voice quickly lost its usual adolescent timbre. Face to face with such an imposing maternal maelstrom he felt like a little boy again. Despite his eighteen years. He tried again to soothe her.

'But Mum it's just a recipe, for God's sake.'

She stopped emptying a bag of apples into the glass bowl on the windowsill. There was a barely audible sigh and her posture softened. Her shoulders dropped. So did her chin. She shook her head piteously.

'It is not just a recipe Nathan.' She didn't turn round. She couldn't even look at him. 'It was a family recipe that your great grandmother perfected years ago, before you were even born. Before I was even born. It's a closely guarded family secret. At least it was. You better put this right boy or I'll never forgive you!'

Nathan was about to protest but she span around and swept past him out of the room. Guilt swelled in his throat because he thought he saw tears in her eyes. The kitchen became chilly.

She'd never called him boy before and there was something worryingly impersonal about it. He simply couldn't understand where the pain was coming from; after all, it was just a recipe. He knew she was proud of her baking abilities and a bit of a local expert, especially when it came to cakes but he had no idea secrets were involved. And yet it had been a long time since Nathan had seen his mother so upset so he knew it was a serious matter to her. He wondered what his father would say when he got home from work later and he felt a shiver pass through him. There was only one thing to do.

It had been another cold day with the countryside bathed in weak winter sunshine. Snow had been forecast all week but as yet, it had not materialized. Nathan slammed the back door and jumped on his little Yamaha. He had been more than comfortable whiling away the afternoon watching TV; the last thing he wanted to do was to ride over to old Mrs

Brody and ask for the recipe back. What the hell was he going to say anyway?

'Sorry Mrs Brody, but the recipe I gave you is an ancient family secret dating back to the Bronze Age and I'm afraid if you've read it I'll have to kill you.'

How preposterous.

He felt embarrassed just thinking about it. Was it really such a big deal that someone else could make a Christmas cake like his mother's? She was always saying how the demand for them at this time of year swamped her. Surely this should have been a bit of a relief if anything. But the harsh tone she had used as he stepped out into the cold persuaded him to kick-start the little engine.

'And don't you come back here unless you've got that recipe, you understand? And make sure she hasn't copied it!'

Nathan shook his head with the tragedy of it all as the two-stroke engine buzzed into life between his legs.

Even though she lived out in the sticks, Mrs Brody was the proverbial village gossip. It seemed to one and all, that her sole purpose in life was to spread rumour. As if this wasn't bad enough, such was her nature that she ignored the pleasant tidings of people's lives in favour of their woes and their troubles, which she would usually embellish with her own bleak view of the world. To see her pull up in her little Morris Minor was like witnessing the arrival of a biblical plague or a conquering force. She'd swoop in, devastate the good cheer of those she encountered and then leave again with a trove full of news and personal information, snippets to twist and corrode before passing them on. Everyone tried to avoid her but Mrs Brody was persistent. She could snare even the most determined of evader unless they were willing to result to downright rudeness and even then, she seemed practically immune, whether through having an extremely thick skin or very poor hearing, no one really knew. She was wiry of body, stern of countenance and had a voice that could grate cheese. And the reason she got hold of so much information was because she was also an accomplished interrogator, which gave rise to her nickname of 'Fraulein Brody'.

Nathan had been surprised when she'd called earlier that afternoon whilst his mother was out and perhaps because he was a teenager he wasn't quite in tune with the social fabric of the older generation to have thought that she may have had a hidden agenda. But it seemed such a small favour. She had asked politely enough for the recipe and although she admitted to being in a hurry, she seemed quite content to wait in the hallway while he copied it onto a piece of paper for her. When Nathan had handed it to her she had crammed the recipe into her coat pocket and said thank you and goodbye with just the briefest of glances at his writing. Nathan had sensed that she wanted to leave before his mother returned from the shops.

A mile out of the village, Nathan turned off the main road into a country lane. His eyes were streaming from the rush of icy air and he found himself blinking constantly to clear his vision. Mrs Brody's meadow-side cottage was a further two miles or thereabouts and it would have been a pleasant ride had it not been so cold. Even in his thermal gloves, Nathan's fingers were already beginning to stiffen and although his full-face helmet kept his head warm, the exposed part of his face felt as though a thousand tiny needles were tattooing frost into it. He pulled over to wipe his eyes.

As he opened the throttle to move off again, the little engine coughed, spluttered and cut out. He pulled out the kick-starter and pumped a few times but the engine failed to catch.

Then he groaned.

Loudly.

He unscrewed the petrol cap and the heady, metallic fumes speared through the cold air and up his nose. He jiggled the bike between his thighs and groaned again when there was no sloshing of liquid. The tank was empty.

Nathan had remembered too late his mental note to go straight to the petrol station on his next ride out. Yesterday's evening blast with friends had been a lot of fun but at some point he had had to switch over to reserve on their way back to the pub. He had returned home after a couple of pints reckoning on having enough juice left to get him to the Esso station in town. He was right, he would have had.

He replaced the petrol cap and considered his options. The closest and warmest one was to go home and face his mother's wrath but her parting expression and the fear of what his father might say made him move swiftly on to the next. To walk back and get petrol would be a five-mile round trip, which would take ages and he wasn't certain of the petrol station's closing time. He didn't want to risk walking all that way only to find it closed. The third option that his numbed initiative came up with was to walk back to the main road and pick up a 419 bus, which would take him to within about half a mile of Mrs Brody's place. He'd have to leave his bike somewhere but he could easily hide it out of sight behind a hedgerow. He realised that he'd still have to get home afterwards but as long as he had that recipe in his hands, he'd be happy and he couldn't care less how long it took. Just so long as he didn't freeze to death on the way. The irony of the unlikely possibility made him smile. That would sure put things into perspective for his mother, he thought.

Cold started nibbling at his toes spurring him to act. He got off the bike, wheeled it around and started off back towards the main road, pushing the Yamaha alongside him. There was no other traffic. The lane was quiet. All he could hear inside his helmet was the muffled sound of his footsteps and the exaggerated volume of the beating of his heart. But at least he was getting warm. After a while, he came across an aluminium gate that barred the way to a field. It seemed a likely place to unburden himself. The field was empty apart from an ancient tree that stood in a sort of hollowed out area several hundred metres away. It had at some point suffered a lightening strike because its branches were without bark and brittle looking and there was a large dead bough rotting on the ground close by. Nathan slid the lever to the side and pushed. The gate swung open. He wheeled the Yamaha in through the opening and across the hard, frosty earth. He continued for a few dozen paces alongside the hedgerow until he was sure the bike couldn't be seen from the road. He lifted it onto its stand and removed the keys from the ignition. He was just applying the steering lock when he became aware of an odd drumming sound. Thinking that something inside the engine was cracking, he whipped off his helmet to better trace the sound. Only it wasn't coming from the bike it was coming from behind him. He turned and saw the enormous barrel-shaped body of a bull bearing down on him like a stream train. For a few seconds, Nathan couldn't move. His mind seemed to have lost the capability of instantly processing what his eyes were seeing. But then as the drumming sound became a thundering sound his mind caught up and his body reacted. He sprang forwards and ran towards the gate like his life depended on it. And it probably did. The approach of thundering hoofs and aggressive snorts from a tonne of bad temper was not to be ignored. The huge Hereford bull was still a little way off when Nathan slid the bolt of the gate back into place and yet he didn't stop running. He didn't know whether bulls were capable of jumping aluminium gates or simply charging them down, he didn't really want to find out and he also didn't want to find out whether bulls liked mangling shiny motorbikes. If they did, there was absolutely nothing he could do to stop it.

A minute or so later, he threw a glance over his shoulder and stopped running. He wasn't being pursued. He took a moment to catch his breath and then continued walking towards the main road and the nearest bus stop.

By the time he reached it, the sun had dropped out of sight in the western sky and the air had become colder. The only parts of Nathan that were cold were his nose and ears but they were so cold that they felt like a sharp tug would snap them off.

Nathan prayed that he hadn't just missed a bus. It wouldn't take long to lose all the heat that his exertions had built up. He looked down the hill at the village a mile or so distant and the soft undulations of the South Downs beyond. He could just make out some coloured tree lights twinkling in a few windows of the closer houses. Christmas was only two weeks away and most of his friends had their decorations up already. Spirals of grey smoke rose from a few chimneys against the pale glow of the horizon, which may have been pink but it was a pink that lacked any warmth.

The minutes ticked by and the light began to fade so that after a while, the cars coming up out of the village had their headlights on. Nathan's attempts to fight off the cold - swaying from side to side and stamping his feet - were futile. Standing still was chilling him to the bone and he wasn't sure how much more he could endure. His teeth had already begun to chatter.

'All this for a stupid recipe,' he grumbled.

After what seemed like an hour, Nathan heard the clattering of a bus's diesel engine climbing slowly up the hill. A moment later, it appeared round a bend, its headlights shining through the dusk like the eyes of a monstrous mechanical caterpillar. Nathan held out his hand and the bus stopped beside him. There was a hydraulic wheeze from its brakes. The door opened and Nathan stepped on board, instantly feeling a wave of glorious warmth embrace him. He smiled gratefully at the driver and removed a glove to find some change.

He fumbled through his pockets then removed his other glove and fumbled again. Coat pockets inside and out, jeans pockets front and back. He concluded with a rapidly forming sense of dread that he'd left home without any money and as if to confirm this, his mind flashed an image into his head of his money sitting on the corner of his desk in his bedroom. Right where he'd left it. He felt stupid and embarrassed but most of all, he didn't want to have to walk back home empty handed. The driver must have interpreted Nathan's expression of embarrassment as genuine rather than someone trying to pull a fast one because his face didn't turn into a scowl. Instead, a teasing smile widened his mouth and the door closed.

'This one's on me,' he said as he found a gear and pulled away from the stop.

'Oh thanks, mate. Thank you so much,' said Nathan, almost melting with gratitude. He ignored the disapproving looks he received from several of the passengers as he walked past them down the bus and took a seat close to the back. He placed his helmet beside him.

Finally, he thought, a stroke of luck. He unzipped his coat and let the warmth from the heaters soothe his half frozen body and within a minute, his jaw ceased its involuntary quivering.

The bus would now take him the majority of the way. He'd get off at Copse Lane, where the old scout hut used to stand before a falling tree destroyed it during last year's great storm and then he'd have about half a mile to walk up Copse Hill to Fraulein Brody's place. The prospect of having to make the long trek home filled Nathan with dread but for the moment, he was happy to relax.

A discarded newspaper on the seat across the aisle caught his eye and he reached over and picked it up. He began turning the crinkly pages scanning the headlines with little or no interest until he came across an interview with one of his favourite singers. They were talking about the upcoming release of a new album followed by a world tour. It wasn't long before Nathan was engrossed.

The bus rumbled on towards the end of its line, stopping now and then to let passengers on and off. They mostly got off and after a while Nathan looked up from the paper and realised that he was one of the last on board. He glanced out the window to see how much further there was to Copse Lane but it was too dark to get a bearing so he thought it wise to ask the driver.

'Excuse me, what's the next stop?'

'Hospital,' replied the driver without taking his eyes from the road.

'What?'

'The hospital.'

'But this is the 419. Doesn't it go straight through to Mayford?' asked Nathan, a little alarmed.

'The 419 does, yes but this is a 419 - A,' replied the driver, emphasising the letter. He tapped the windscreen to point out the bus's illuminated designation. 'And every other hour the 419 - A turns off and goes to the hospital instead.'

'Damn! I wanted Copse Lane.'

'You should've said. I would've told you.'

Nathan could have kicked himself for not paying attention. He should have noticed that. God, the amount of bad luck he was having on this stupid little mission was unbelievable. Fortunately for Nathan, the driver was already filled with the festive spirit because he offered to drop him off right away. Nathan wrapped himself up again and retrieved his helmet from the seat as the bus pulled over. He thanked the driver for his kindness and wished him a Happy Christmas.

'You too,' replied the driver. The door closed and the hammering of the diesel engine increased as the driver throttled away. The bus soon disappeared over a crest in the road and took its noise with it.

Nathan was standing on a quiet country road bordered both sides by overgrown ditches and high hedges. In both directions he saw nothing. No lights from houses, no headlights from cars and no streetlights. The silence was eerie. It felt like the middle of nowhere. The only thing he could discern in the gloom was the outline of the hedgerows against the sky. There were no stars twinkling overhead and so Nathan guessed that it had clouded over. With no footpath to walk along and no street lighting Nathan knew that he wasn't wearing ideal clothing for night-time road walking - dark blue and black were risky choices – and so he walked briskly but carefully as he retraced the bus's route back up to the main road.

Now he either had to find another bus stop and wait for a 419 that was going through to Mayford or he had to walk all the way to Mrs Brody's. He estimated it to be close to a mile, including the walk up Copse Hill. But Nathan was tired of walking. It was cold and he was fed up with things going wrong. First running out of petrol, then nearly being trampled by a bull, then almost freezing to death and then getting on the wrong bus, which he wouldn't have been able to get on at all if the driver hadn't been such a nice guy because like an idiot he'd left his wallet at home!

Jesus!

He was certainly paying dearly for making a copy of that damned recipe.

It occurred to him as he continued walking, using the grass verge as his guide, that he had no choice but to go all the way on foot. After all, he had no money for a bus. And to expect another free ride was frankly asking too much. Especially with the day he was having. And anyway, he decided he couldn't face waiting in the cold again for however long it would take a 419 to come. At least if he was walking he wouldn't freeze. Accepting this as his short-term fate, Nathan relaxed a little and set his brain to thinking. What he really needed was a shortcut.

He was familiar with the road he was on however, it was so dark he couldn't determine exactly how far to the hospital he had got before getting off the bus. The road didn't have any obvious landmarks and the borders were high enough that Nathan couldn't see over them to gain a bearing from the surrounding countryside. Assuming the worst, he mentally pinpointing his location as being closer to the hospital than he'd like, and then he tried to remember if there was a shortcut he could take, a public footpath a bridleway, anything. After a few minutes, a shortcut did come to mind and just as Nathan was wondering how far he had to walk before reaching it, the high beams of an approaching vehicle silhouetted a crest in the road ahead. Nathan quickly stepped up onto the grassy verge and got out of the road as the car came into view, headlights blazing like interrogators lamps. The speed it was going unnerved him and Nathan involuntarily took a further step back.

And lost his footing.

The car roared past in a burst of noise and light and was soon swallowed up by a bend in the road. Silence returned. But that extra step of caution had sent

Nathan sliding down into the soggy ditch and the freezing water at its bottom instantly seeped into his boots and made the denim of his jeans stick to his lower legs like ice-cold bandages.

Nathan couldn't believe it. He cursed the speeding car and then cursed his mother. He then cursed the recipe and Mrs Brody, whom he blamed for started the whole affair, and as he emptied the ditch water from his crash helmet he cursed the car again.

He was fuming and ranting as he pulled himself out of the ditch, fingers raw as they clutched icy cold grass. He decided that he was quite possibly having the worst evening of his entire life. Back up on the road, his feet squelched in his boots as he walked along in a shroud of misery.

'What the hell else is going to happen tonight?'

Thick flakes of snow began to float down from the sky as if some divine power had just shaken their snow globe.

The short cut that Nathan's memory provided was a good one but it wasn't via a public right of way. It would involve sneaking through a farmyard. Then, after crossing a couple of fields, he would be within a stone's throw of Mrs Brody's cottage.

The snow continued falling heavily, big soft flakes that soon covered the hedges and trees like a layer of fluffy white down. The roads had been gritted daily all week so for the moment, they remained clear. Apart from the cold below his knee-line Nathan thought it had actually warmed up a little. But it was probably just the walking that had warmed him up.

It wasn't too long before he arrived at his shortcut - the farm entrance. With snow covering every surface, darkness had been forced to make a minor retreat. It was far from light but it was at least possible to see and as Nathan peered into the yard, it looked exactly as he remembered. Years ago, he had been friends with one of the farmer's sons - Charlie - and had played there often and because of that, he knew that at the back of the yard behind the barns and sheds was a gate that led out onto fields. And across those fields was Copse Hill where Mrs Brody lived.

A wide concrete driveway lay beside a red brick farmhouse set back from the road. It opened onto a large, cluttered yard. With the snow aiding vision, Nathan was easily able to pick out the outbuildings and barns where the farm equipment and vehicles were kept.

Several lights were on in the farmhouse but the yard was quiet and Nathan hoped that he wouldn't be seen. He would be trespassing on private property after all. A clatter of crockery and clink of cutlery came from the house and Nathan pictured the scene in the kitchen; hopefully, they were all about to sit down to dinner. Apart from that there was absolute silence.

Adrenalin pumping through Nathan's body acted like antifreeze. He actually felt hot.

He crept into the yard and moved quickly past the farmhouse and the first outbuilding where a Land Rover was parked. His footsteps made muffled scrunching sounds that seemed to him loud enough for those indoors to hear. He continued on past a large barn that he assumed, from the smell within, was filled with straw or hay. A movement from inside stopped him dead in his tracks. His breath held tightly in his lungs. His ears strained to identify the sound, to convert it into an image in his head, to tell him whether or not he'd been discovered and would have to start explaining his presence. But the sound came again and Nathan identified it as a hoof scraping on a concrete floor. He breathed again and continued onwards.

Away from the house, he moved a little quicker, a little easier, eager to find the gate that would signal safety. As he rounded the tractor shed, he heard straw rustling in its dark depths. Then, he heard a low growl. A black and white shape emerged into the snowy gloom and Nathan saw a dog approaching, its teeth bared in a warning snarl. His stomach lurched.

'Good dog, good dog,' he whispered as calmly as his fear would permit. 'It's ok, I'm not going to bother you so please, please don't bother me.' Nathan made calming movements with his hands but with a helmet in one of them, it must have seemed to the dog like he was being goaded. The dog continued advancing, snarling, it's head low, it's eyes fixed on the stranger in its yard. Nathan felt nervous sweat deep inside his layers of clothing. He threw a glance up past the shed and saw his gate to freedom. He quickly calculated the distance. The dog let go with a warning bark that echoed around the farmyard like a gunshot. Nathan sprinted towards the gate as fast as he could and the dog took off after him, barking aggressively. Nathan threw himself over the gate in a sort of diving roll, tucking his chin into his chest and rounding his back as he went. He released his helmet as he landed cleanly on his shoulder and his momentum brought him quickly back to his feet. He scooped up his helmet again and ran across the field while the dog continued barking at the gate. When he was a third of the way across he heard a gruff voice call out for the dog to shut up.

He was laughing aloud when he climbed over the gate into the next field. He was out of breath and his lungs were burning from running in the freezing air but he felt warmer than he had since getting off the bus. His feet were still a bit squidgy and he sensed the onset of a blister or two but overall, Nathan felt exhilarated. He hadn't had as much fun in ages. It had certainly beaten watching TV all afternoon.

Ten minutes later, the lights of a cottage came into view. They were the other side of the hedge that bordered the top of the field, close to the left hand corner. Nathan hoped that it was Mrs Brody's although now that he was closing in on his target, he began to feel nervous about explaining his reason for turning up on her doorstep. The gate that would let him out onto the lane was in the right hand corner of the field so Nathan had a slight detour before he emerged onto the partly snow-covered tarmac. Another two minutes and he was standing outside the little cottage, with Mrs Brody's Morris Minor parked outside its front door.

He stood outside her gate and put his helmet on the ground. Almost immediately, icy fingers began to work their way through his layers of clothing, placing a chill back inside his body. Nathan wanted to hurry up and get this over with before he froze to death but he just couldn't think of what to say to the woman. He whispered a few opening lines to himself but they all sounded so ridiculous that he discarded them with contempt. He looked around for inspiration but the remote cottage and the white landscape offered none. He wondered if his mother would still be angry with him if he went home empty handed. Had she calmed down? Was she waiting to apologise for overreacting earlier? He thought it unlikely.

Nathan didn't know what time it was but he suspected his father was home by now and had probably been told what had happened. He wondered whether his dad was just as furious with him or if he considered the whole thing daft. Perhaps he followed the same logic as Nathan – it's just a recipe. Then again, perhaps not. Could he lie and tell his mother that he watched Mrs Brody tear up the recipe and toss it into the fire? Again, Nathan thought probably not.

He thought about the last few hours and the journey that had brought him to this point and he felt strangely proud of himself. His mother had asked him to do a pretty simple thing and yet, it had turned out to be anything but simple. It had turned into an obstacle-ridden adventure. And yet, he had overcome each obstacle without too much difficulty. How could he endure all that had happened only to back out at the very end? All the hassles would have been for nothing.

Nathan made up his mind. He took a deep, bolstering lungful of frozen air and strode in through the gate. He hadn't a clue what he was going to say or how Mrs Brody might react but he knew he had to try. He moved silently up to the rounded shape of the car, its cold metal surfaces obscured beneath an inch thick white blanket and suddenly the door of the cottage opened. It surprised him so much he almost squealed. His reaction was quick though and he dropped to one knee behind the little car, hoping that Mrs Brody hadn't seen him. Even if she hadn't, she could surely hear his heart banging against his chest. Her footsteps scrunched in the snow and Nathan squeezed his eyes shut and prayed that she wasn't about to retrieve something from the car boot. Her scream of surprise was surely going to pierce the air any second. She unlocked the passenger door and reached in to take something from the seat. She then slammed the door, locked it again and turned quickly back towards the cottage, mumbling something about the dreadful snow.

Nathan peered around the rear corner of the Morris and saw that she was carrying a coat, the same one she'd been wearing earlier that day when she had stood in his hallway. He wondered if the recipe was still in its pocket. Just before she closed her front door something caught the hallway light as it fell from the coat onto the doormat. Nathan stared through the gloom and decided it was a crumpled piece of paper.

'No, it couldn't be,' he thought to himself. 'I'm not that lucky.'

Excitement that he might well indeed be that lucky gave him courage and lead him forward past the car. He stepped onto the porch and bent down to pick up the piece of paper and saw at once, even in the poor light, that it was the recipe he'd written out that afternoon. His frozen lips cracked as his mouth widened into a grin and he felt an instant euphoria. Now, his mother could rest happy and forgive him and the whole episode could be forgotten. He felt so relieved and happy that he wanted to whoop for joy and dance through the pristine snow but then he remembered his long, cold journey back home and his happiness shrunk. He folded the piece of paper and placed it in his jacket pocket just as the door opened again. Light fell on him exposing his presence to Mrs

Brody. She looked at him with a mixture of suspicion and surprise.

Desperately hoping his initiative would conjure an excuse for his being there, Nathan couldn't prevent himself from gazing like a rabbit caught in headlights at the lines and wrinkles that criss-crossed her unkind face. Her thin, grey eyebrows arched impatiently.

'I sincerely hope you are here for a reason, young man.' Her dark, piercing eyes made Nathan nervous and he stuttered something unintelligible to her.

'I beg your pardon,' she demanded.

'I...ran out of petrol.' It was the only thing that came to his numbed mind but he felt a spark of confidence when he realised that it wasn't a complete lie.

'You ran out of petrol? A fine night you chose to do that. Come in before you let all my heat out.' She moved her thin frame aside and he felt again, the bliss of warmth envelope him. 'So, you thought you would knock on my door,' she said. Nathan didn't know whether she was asking him why he had knocked on her door but with the warmth exacerbating his tiredness together with the knowledge that he had at last got what he came for he felt like being direct.

'You couldn't give me a lift home could you?' he asked, in as pleasant a manner as he could. 'The roads are still okay.' He knew they were only partially covered at the moment but if it continued snowing like it was, he suspected Mrs Brody might struggle to get back up Copse Hill. He held her stern gaze but attempted to dissipate it with a warm friendly smile. Her gaze remained stern though as she considered his request. It was clear she loathed the thought of going back out into the cold.

'I suppose as you did something for me earlier, I could do something for you now,' she said in a business-like manner. 'I'll just be a minute.'

It was all Nathan could do to stop himself from punching the air.

The First Impression for Mr King

A faint click started Tony's day. A faint click followed immediately by four short beeps, like Morse code dots. It continued with four more. Then four more. It had an incessant quality. Unrelenting. Like it would go on all day if it could.

Tony remained still, listening and wondering why it sounded different this morning. It was the same alarm, from the same phone and it was about the same distance from his pillow. But somehow it was less intrusive, easier on the ear as if the volume had been turned down a notch or two. The answer came to him a second later. It was because he was in a bigger room. A much bigger room. More space for the sound to fill. To dissipate. Three mornings ago, it had woken him up in his old room at his parent's house, a room of about twelve square feet and in comparison, the electronic beeping had sounded like a lorry reversing, filling the space with its sleep-shattering staccato.

Tony reached for the phone and silenced it.

06:45.

Perfect.

The alarm hadn't actually woken him. He'd been awake for the last hour. He'd been enjoying the peace, relaxing in his new bed, in his new room, in his new home, thinking of the day ahead. It was a big day, first day on the new job and he wanted everything to go well. He was excited but nervous. He pushed himself up onto his elbows and peered around the room. He grinned. If he didn't know otherwise, he'd never guess he was lying in bed above a garage. Compared to the former council flat he'd been sharing in town with his ex - Dinah - it was a penthouse. But then it was a four-car garage he was above. The apartment, the studio, maisonette or whatever term an estate agent would use to sell it was quite frankly beautiful.

The garage block was three times wider than it was deep with four doors for four vehicles. There was a dividing wall down the centre for support that continued up into the apartment and the roof space above. Two wide dormer windows faced front and two faced back with a small window in each gable end. All together they gave the south-facing apartment an abundance of light. A staircase led from a side door in the right rear corner of the garage up to the first floor. To one side of the centre wall was the bedroom and bathroom, fully furnished and seemingly with no expense spared. The bathroom was finished in white tiling, mirrors and chrome fixtures of high quality. A wide archway in the centre wall led to the sitting area and kitchen. The sitting area was designated by two comfy red fabric sofas placed at right angles to each other, effectively squaring off one corner of the space. There was large flat-screen TV and DVD player plus Internet access. A coffee table and another smaller table on which sat a reading lamp offered a touch of homeliness. Next to one of the sofas and set between the front windows was a compact dining table with four chairs and built against the end wall was a well-appointed kitchenette complete with breakfast bar and a couple of stools. A plain but far from inexpensive beige carpet covered the floor throughout and simple white blinds hung at the windows. The walls were painted something akin to magnolia but not quite. Tony hadn't stayed in many hotel rooms but what he was looking at was nicer than those he had.

Anyway enough dallying. Time to get up. Tony threw off the covers and walked naked into the bathroom, his toes enjoying the rich fibres of the carpet.

An hour and fifteen minutes later he was downstairs in the garage having showered, dressed and taken a light breakfast of tea and toast. He flicked a switch on the wall and half a dozen neon strips blinked into life, bathing the interior of the garage in a stark white wash.

His excitement jumped at what he saw.

The left flank of the car in front of him seemed as long as the side of a small ocean-going vessel. The highest point of its beautifully contoured, piano-black bonnet was almost level with his chest. Magnificent was the word that came to mind. The winged 'B' on top of the radiator grill told him he was looking at a Bentley but he hadn't a clue which model it was. It took seven strides to reach the rear of the car, which was just as stirring with its graceful curves and two fat tailpipes.

Excitement didn't begin to describe what Tony was feeling.

But he was also nervous.

The most impressive car he had driven to date was a twelve-year-old Jaguar XJ. Two years ago at his last job, a new customer had come in and part-exchanged it for a mundane but economically sensible Mondeo. As shop driver, it had been Tony's job to deliver the new car to their home and of course, this came with the bonus of having to drive the Jag back to the Ford dealership. Tony had risked getting an ear bashing from his boss by taking the scenic route back but it would've been worth it because the Jag had been a dream to drive.

But this Bentley was in another league altogether.

Beside the Bentley sat a BMW 4x4. An X5. It was shorter than its neighbour by almost a metre, higher by a margin but completely void of any elegance. Standing beside something else, it would probably have stood out because an X5 is a nice car but next to the Bentley it looked like a boulder on wheels, albeit a sculpted one. It too was black but somehow less so and probably not just because of its light covering of dirty rain spots.

Tony couldn't wait to see what the other side of the dividing wall would reveal and he tracked around the BMW and passed through the archway. The first thing he saw was an empty space where he was expecting another car, an area of smooth bare concrete with one or two dried drops of oil in evidence. He was mildly disappointed. But then in the next space he saw a dustsheet draped across a low sleek shape and his disappointment evaporated like petrol fumes in the sun. He lifted a corner of the sheet and saw an unfamiliar name in chrome script against the deep blue paintwork. Gordon Keeble. The chrome bumper and pressed steel wheel with its three eared centre lock nut made him assume he was looking at a classic from the '50s or '60s.

Whatever it was, it was clearly very pretty.

He lifted the sheet a little further down and cupped his hand to the driver's window. He saw swathes of padded black leather, an array of white on black dials - big and small - several rows of toggle switches in the centre console and an enormous thin-rimmed, triple-spoke wooden steering wheel. It looked amazing and the prospect of getting to drive such a beautiful car made his mouth water. He didn't know whether it was in his job description to do so but he hoped it was. The V8 badge low down on the front wing had him practically drooling.

Tony carefully let the dustsheet fall and took a moment to consider his new job while he looked around the rest of the garage. These cars were now his responsibility. It was now down to him to keep them clean, serviceable and road legal and apart from the remedial routine tasks of checking fluid levels and adding where necessary, all maintenance was to be taken care of by those entrusted by his new employer – Mr King.

What could be better? Driving expensive cars without having to pick up the bill.

Was this a dream job or what?

The rest of the garage was routine. The Gordon Keeble side had a large red tool chest on top of a sturdy bench, which ran along the length of the rear wall. Hanging above this from numerous hooks and nails were various basic tools from the hammer, pliers and screwdriver families. They looked largely undisturbed. There were numerous shelves on which sat various cans of oil, cleaners, aerosols and polishes. Cloths and rags made from old towels and bed sheets sat in a multi-coloured heap under the bench, as did an assortment of car-cleaning paraphernalia such as buckets, sponges, brushes and chamois leathers. The Bentley side had an extension ladder hanging on wall brackets down one side as well as a small stepladder and a green garden hose neatly wound on its reel, which was fixed to the wall just inside the opening doors. An industrial-sized vacuum cleaner and an old plastic dustbin completed the equipment list. Everything needed to valet a car. Or three.

A good first impression was important to Tony and he had decided last night that his first task of his first day would be to ensure that when he collected Mr King from the airport later that afternoon, the car he arrived in would be spotless. He was nervous about this encounter because he had yet to meet the man who would be paying his wages. The chauffeur vacancy had come about unexpectedly early last week while Mr King had been away on business and it had therefore been left to Mrs King to quickly find a replacement. With no real time to widely advertise the post, she had put notes in the windows of the village newsagent and on the advertising board of the supermarket in the nearby town of Lymbridge. Not surprisingly, with such a small net cast, there hadn't been many responses for a "live-in chauffeur" but with Tony recently separated from his partner of four years and forced to take refuge back at his parents home, he had been only too keen to apply after the job had caught his mother's eye whilst she had been on her weekly shopping trip.

According to Mrs King, Tony had been one of only three initial respondents and by far the most suitable. He had plenty of driving experience and also, as she put it, 'a respectable appearance.' She said her husband would insist she select someone possessed with a certain level of decorum and dignity and apparently Tony had ticked those boxes. She had offered him the job right then and there. That was last Thursday.

A row of four white switches on the wall operated the up-and-over garage doors and Tony pressed the one he thought would correspond with the door behind the Bentley. He guessed right. An electric motor whirred and a clatter of metal accompanied the rising of the first door as its pulley mechanism drew the heavy panel of wood up and over the rear of the car. Morning sunlight flooded in and added a little warmth to the neon strips' cool, sterile glare.

A brick-surfaced area about the size of a tennis court fronted the garage. The bricks were arranged in a herringbone pattern and had a small metal drain at their centre, which was by design a fraction lower than the surrounding edges. The forecourt gave onto a gravelled driveway that swept past a bank of tall conifers and up to the main house, which was from this position, out of sight. Herbaceous borders and well-established oaks and beeches hemmed in a garden that was well tended. A light dew glistened across the lawns like condensation on an ice cold Mojito but the air was warm and sweet-scented from the lavender and honeysuckle that grew close by.

Tony took a small key from his pocket and unlocked a sturdy metal box fixed to the wall at the rear of the garage. It contained numerous sets of keys hanging on small hooks. Each car had two sets and each set was on the ring of a black fob with the corresponding maker's badge. Tony was intrigued to see only one set with an Aston Martin fob and his inner child instantly put two and two together and assumed that the empty space next to the Gordon Keeble was only temporary. A car was away being serviced or repaired. And an Aston Martin, no less. At least, that's what he hoped.

This job was getting better by the minute.

He selected a key ring with a "B" on it and relocked the box. He then pushed a button on the electronic fob and the Bentley unlocked itself with a silent flash of orange from each corner. His heartbeat rose from a canter to a gallop as he opened the weighty door and settled himself into the sumptuous driver's seat. It was like nothing he'd experienced before. The soft leather with its unmistakably expensive aroma, the stitching along the seams of the seats and the dash and even the steering wheel, the deep luxurious carpet, the mirror-like finish of the walnut veneer. One word. Opulent. Tony felt as though he'd climbed the social ladder simply by getting in.

He put the key in the ignition, low and right and, after checking the transmission was in PARK, gave it a twist. The starter motor whirred briefly and the engine caught and settled instantly into a fast idle, it's many moving parts filling the garage with a smooth mechanical purr. Tony pulled the door to and the sound stopped. Completely. As though someone had just switched the volume off. Or the engine had just died. But the delicate needle in the right hand dial told him that the huge engine was still running at a fraction over 600rpm.

Tony checked his distances, took a deep breath, selected reverse with the chrome detailed gearlever and let off the parking brake. He edged the car back out into the sunlight with a surgeon-like precision, stopping somewhere above the drain on the forecourt. After switching the engine off, he suddenly realised how tense he was. Every muscle in his body was wired and taught and he got out and shook himself all over, like a dog drying itself after a dip in a pool. For a few seconds after his head swam and he saw spots before his eyes but it went a long way to releasing the tension. He was going to have to get used to these cars quickly if he was to drive them with confidence.

The sound of crunching on the gravel made him turn around. A mature gent in faded brown corduroys and a blue Barbour waistcoat pushed a wheelbarrow onto the forecourt. On his feet were a pair of sturdy old wellies and on his head sat a well-worn brown tweed flat cap.

'Aye-up,' he called. 'You must be the new driver.' His accent was rounded and rural with vowel sounds that seemed to remain in the back of his throat.

'Morning,' said Tony. 'That I am.'

'Pleased to meet you.' He set down the wheelbarrow and wiped a hand down his waistcoat before extending it to Tony and introducing himself as Henry, the man who kept the grounds in order. His forearms were thin and wiry but the muscles moved beneath the burned toffee skin like mooring ropes tightening around a bollard. They shook briefly. It was a formality. The old guard welcoming the new.

'And I'm Tony.' Tony put Henry close to retirement age and for that he looked in pretty good physical shape. However, his skin, or at least what Tony could see of it on his hands, face, and neck looked as though it might have been second hand when the man was born. The man's hand had felt more like tree bark than flesh. Henry's face was the same colour as his arms and it was a well-proportioned face with a square jaw line, a proud nose and glittering eyes. Or rather eye. His left eye didn't follow the movements of its neighbour and although its colour was no different Tony assumed it was glass. He found himself looking at it just a little too much even though he tried not to.

Henry removed his cap and brushed his forearm across a damp brow. It was only a little after eight but it was clear from his ruddy complexion that he'd been toiling for a while already. He then asked, 'So, you settled in all right up there?'

'Yes, I think so.' Tony replied.

'Pretty little flat isn't it?'

'Little? I feel like I'm staying in a fancy hotel room. I reckon it's the nicest place I've ever lived and I'm going to be very comfy up there.'

'Sure you will. 'Course, this was where the stable block was back in the day, you know?'

'Really?'

'Oh yeah. It's been completely rebuilt since then, mind; that's why it doesn't look very old but the original foundations are still there.' Henry moved forward and began indicating certain points with pointed fingers. 'Would've likely been only two openings instead of four, wider of course, and the back would've been open like the front so's the horses could've turned the carriages around before being unhitched. You go and see the rose garden and you'll know where all that manure went.'

'Who said recycling was a modern day thing, eh?' quipped Tony.

'So, I see you're getting stuck in already,' said Henry, with a nod towards the Bentley. 'Beauty isn't she?'

Tony agreed that she was but added that he was a little nervous driving such an expensive car.

'I thought you chauffeurs were used to driving such things,' said Henry. Tony wasn't sure but he thought he detected a whiff of condescension in Henry's tone. Not wanting to give the impression he wasn't up to the job he went on the defensive.

'Well, I've driven plenty of Jags and such but it just so happens that this is my first Bentley.' It wasn't exactly true but then it wasn't exactly a lie either. Henry then asked whether Tony had seen the Gordon Keeble and informed him that it was Mr King's pride and joy.

'I've never known a man love a car as much. Treats it like a mistress, he does. Never takes it out unless it's sunny and always gets it looking spic and span before covering it over. Shows it at rallies and enters it into competitions and so forth. I think it's won a couple too and even been featured in a classic car magazine. You know there were only about a hundred of them made,' he added.

'Really? So it must be worth a pretty penny, then.' And Tony thought he was nervous about driving the Bentley. At least that wasn't irreplaceable.

'More than I would ever spend on a car, that's for sure. Tell you what, young man,' said Henry, running fingers through his short, wiry salt and pepper hair before putting his cap back on. In truth it was mostly salt but there was a little pepper remaining at the back. 'I've got a kettle and some digestives in my shed. Fancy a cuppa?'

Tony could still taste the cup he'd had with breakfast and he wasn't a big tea drinker at the best of times. He didn't want to appear unsociable but he wanted to get on with cleaning the Bentley. His nerves needed settling and that would only happen once he'd got himself ahead of the day's schedule.

'I'd love one,' he replied, 'but I really need to get this washed and dried before the sun gets too high and too hot. How about elevenses?

'Sounds good.' Henry picked up the wheelbarrow handles. 'I'll stop by later then. If you need anything, I'm not far away. Just holler.'

'Great. Thanks Henry.'

Henry turned the barrow around and moved off the way he had come. His crunching on the gravel soon faded as he disappeared out of sight around the bank of conifers.

Tony stood for a moment and listened to the summer morning. The birds were the dominant sound, a plethora of warbles and whistles and tweets coming from every direction, near and far. But in that moment, there were other sounds - the faint jet-scream of an airplane cruising at high altitude, the rich tone of a biggish dog like a Labrador or Alsatian barking playfully somewhere not far off, a car stopping and starting as it made its way along the quiet lane a couple of hundred metres away and an unseen tractor operating in a field that was way beyond the vibrant trees that bordered the grounds of his new place of residence. So many sounds and yet such peace. The nearby honeysuckle buzzed as though it had a large electric current running through it and Tony watched as numerous bees floated from one flower to the next in their quest for pollen.

What a way to start the day. It sure beat his former daily commute across Lymbridge in a crowded bus with school kids shouting in his ears.

It was no great hardship to give the Bentley a thorough wash. In fact Tony rather enjoyed it. He had grown quite adept at cleaning cars while working at Ford's and he had learned that thorough meant wiping down the inside edges of the doors and sills too. Getting in and out of a clean car that still had dirty sills was a sure-fire way of spoiling the hems of trousers.

Once the car was rinsed, Tony leathered off the paintwork. Then he brushed some blackener on the tyre walls. Then he stood back and admired his handiwork.

Yes, the car was showroom clean.

He then gave the foot wells inside a brief going over with the vacuum to pick up a few specks of dirt. They didn't really need it but he thought he might as well while he was about it. It was a little after ten-thirty when he returned the vacuum to the garage. Hot coffee and biscuits were on his mind but he thought it wise to pull the Bentley back under cover from passing birds. Tony knew that a freshly cleaned car was an irresistible target for a bird with either a grudge against humanity or a cruel sense of humour. More than once it had happened that no sooner had he turned his back than his hard work had been ruined by an incoming streak of white dung. And with all these trees around he didn't care for his odds.

A twist of the key brought the Bentley back to life. Tony was about to pull forward and surgically re-implant the wide car back into its space through the not-so-wide doorframe when he happened to glance at the fuel gauge. It was just over a quarter full. He didn't have to take out a calculator to figure the car wouldn't make it to Heathrow and back on what was there and so once again, his cantering heartbeat became a gallop as he realised the necessity to go out and get a fill-up. And he may as well do it sooner rather than later. And if he were quick, he'd still be able to make elevenses with Henry.

Mrs King had already provided him with the charge card for their account at the Lymbridge Shell station. She had given it to him on Saturday along with the keys to the garage and a list of 'dos and don'ts'. It was an efficient system that didn't require their driver to carry any cash. The card simply recorded each transaction at the pumps and at the end of every month their bank account was debited for the total. All Tony had to do was remember to keep the card in a pocket and the PIN number in his head.

He ran up to the apartment to collect the petrol card, which he slid in to his wallet. At least by keeping it there, he knew he'd never leave home without it. He locked the door to the apartment and then, having pressed the switch on the wall to lower the garage door, he ducked beneath it moments before it came to a stop and locked itself shut.

Tony got in the Bentley and started it up again. He took a deep breath. This was it. Here he goes. Tony Garwood behind the wheel of one of the world's most prestigious cars.

The forecourt was plenty wide enough to turn around and after a clean three-point turn, Tony followed the gravel driveway back round towards the house, past its sunlit Georgian façade with its wide-stepped portico and sandstone columns and then onwards between the expansive lawns and elegantly shaped evergreen shrubs towards the iron-gated entrance.

He was amazed at how well the car was insulated. Outside, the tyres would be scrunching and rattling on the gravel and probably making enough noise that wherever he was, Henry would be able to hear him leaving but inside the plush cabin with the windows sealed, Tony heard nothing. No tyre noise, no engine noise, nothing. It was like sitting in the reading room of an exclusive old-school gentlemen's club that just happened to be drifting through the countryside.

Tony turned left out of the gate between high sandstone pillars and accelerated gently down the lane towards the little village of Poe. Patches of sunlight filtering through the verdant trees flitted across the windscreen like a succession of flashbulbs going off, as if he was passing a long line of paparazzi. The Bentley was a doddle to drive. Like the Jaguar he had once driven, Tony felt that all he had to do was to keep the thing on course. Its large torque-rich engine and smooth automatic gearbox did all the work. It was like steering a small ship along a narrow waterway, its buoyant bulk smoothing out the ripples on the water.

He took extra care on the way into the village where the lane narrows between a row of old cottages on one side and the church entrance on the other. For about twenty metres, flinty walls ran precariously close to the road on both sides and in many places along their flanks scratches of colour spoke of vehicles having got too close.

The village stores at the heart of Poe, both literally and figuratively, looked like an appealing watercolour with its hanging baskets of Lobelias and white-framed windows. As Tony drove by, he saw Danny Goldman, a fellow dart player from his pub's Friday night team emerge from the shop and hurry towards his parked van. He was carrying a newspaper and a loaf of bread in his arms. Tony found himself having to resist the temptation to sound the horn and wave in a mock regal manner, all nostrils and false smiles. After all, personal chauffeurs like butlers, should exercise a stoic dignity and not give in to signalling at their friends like attention-seeking adolescents. Even if that's what they were.

Clear of Poe, the road unravelled itself for almost a mile before reaching the fringes of Lymbridge. A pair of long straights separated by a deceivingly long curve was too much temptation and as Tony came onto the first straight he flexed his right foot and allowed the Bentley to flex its muscle. Now he could hear the engine's voice. A subtle roar from somewhere out front was joined by a deep bellow from the exhaust, as the roadside scenery quickly became a green blur. The car hit ninety without even trying and after slowing for the curve Tony opened the taps a second time to brush triple figures before slowing again for the tighter corner that marked the unofficial boundary of Lymbridge. A minute later, he pulled onto a four-island forecourt and stopped at one of the pumps. He was grinning from ear to ear.

He was still grinning from ear to ear six minutes later when he handed the cashier the petrol card. Tony was a little shocked at how much it cost to fill the car but he was extremely glad that it wasn't coming out of his pocket. The pump had delivered £107.42 before deciding there was no room in the Bentley's one hundred-litre tank for any more. The cashier handed back the card and instructed Tony in a bored tone that he needed to place the card into the reader on the counter and type in his PIN code. Tony did. He was then given a receipt and bade farewell.

He took the drive home a little more sedately paying more attention to where the car sat between the centre line and the verge. Keeping his eyes fixed on the road ahead, he positioned the car as close to the verge as he thought safe before checking his nearside mirror to see how close he actually was. He tried this several times and found that he could judge the car's width pretty well. The future was undoubtedly going to bring with it regular trips up to the crowded streets of London and Tony wanted to get the feel of exactly where the extremities of this five-metre long limousine were.

When he pulled up in front of the garage the clock on the Bentley's dash told him it was a smidge past eleven ten. Ten minutes late for coffee and biscuits. He hoped Henry wouldn't mind.

He got out the car and was about to hurry inside to unlock the garage again when Henry appeared on the forecourt behind him.

'Aye-up,' he said. 'Thought I heard you.'

'Hi Henry,' said Tony. 'I just popped out to fill her up ready for later.'

'Reckoned that's where you'd gone off to. Still feel like that coffee?'

'You bet. Let me just go in and open up and put her away. Just in case, you know?' Tony glanced up at the sky as if the birds were watching, waiting.

'You can open up from in there, you know?' said Henry, indicating the car.

'I can?' replied Tony.

'Sure,' said Henry pulling open the passenger door. 'All the cars have a remote so you can drive on in without having to get out.' He reached into the storage unit beneath the central armrest and produced a small black box about the size of a matchbox. It had a single white button in its centre and when Henry pressed it, the left hand garage door began its brief journey back up inside.

'Nice,' said Tony, genuinely surprised. 'That's ideal. Thanks for showing me.'

Henry raised a grubby 'think-nothing-of-it' hand in response.

Tony got in the car and, aware that he had an audience who may or may not report to his employers as to how the new guy was coping, returned the Bentley to the garage as easily as if he'd been doing it for months. He rejoined Henry on the forecourt a minute later feeling a lot more confident about driving the big, expensive car. It was only when his thoughts returned to Mr King that he felt a curious apprehension, like a pendulum was quivering on a seismometer deep inside his stomach. He had no idea why the prospect of meeting the man should concern him so.

Giving a sort of tour guide's commentary as they went, Henry led the way up to and around the corner of the house. He informed Tony that the trees sheltering the garage block from the house were red cedar conifers and old English yews. He said that some of the yew trees were over three hundred years old and singled out the granddaddy of them all, which stood resplendent on its own in the middle of the lawns, its truck and lower boughs looking like the muscled thighs of a huge dinosaur, its dark green foliage creating a vast circle of shade on the ground beneath. The house was built in the Georgian style but Henry wasn't sure if it was from that period or if it was built later. It had wide sash windows, which looked all the better for still being wood and not plastic replacements and a wide front door with a vast decorative fanlight above. Tall brick chimneys pointed skywards at either end of the shallow pitched roof. To Tony, Georgian or not, it was an impressive pile. The east-facing front and the south side of the house were relatively open with sweeping lawns and shrubbery giving way to open pasture beyond a line of ancient oaks but the rear of the house and the north side had more going on. There were herbaceous borders and hedges and pebbled pathways, outhouses and garden sheds and a vegetable patch. Henry led Tony through the walled rose garden where banks of flowers and arches of trellis entwined with beautiful colour gave the area a heady concoction of fragrances. He made a passing comment on what the horse manure had achieved over the years, which they both found amusing. After that they came to a nursery area where paving slabs ran around and in between two wooden-framed greenhouses, each about six metres long. The air smelled of compost and tomato vines.

One of the greenhouses was filled with hope and energy; it's long wooden benches laden with trays of potted seedlings and the green shoots of infant plant life. It was humid inside and earthy and there was a sense of expectation in the air, of good things to come. A traffic light of colour covered several tomato vines down one side. The other greenhouse was filled with memories and junk. A few clay pots containing dead plants sat on an otherwise empty bench with a broken hand trowel for company, its handle rotted through and snapped. Beneath the bench numerous screwed up empty compost bags filled a rusted wheelbarrow, its tyre baggy and airless and brittle. The air was dry, dusty like old bones.

A white plastic kettle sat on the bench with a collection of stained mugs nearby. There was also a tartan patterned tin which Tony assumed contained biscuits. Beside it were a box of teabags and a jar of coffee, as well as a carton of milk and a container of sugar. A thumbed copy of the Daily Mail was folded quarter ways showing a crossword that was half complete. A couple of striped folding picnic chairs waited to be sat in.

Henry suggested Tony make use of one as he switched on the kettle and went about making two mugs of coffee. He hadn't asked if that's what Tony wanted but Tony would've preferred coffee to tea anyway.

'This seems like a lot of garden for one man to look after,' said Tony, easing into one of the chairs. 'You do it all yourself?'

'Mostly,' replied Henry. 'Mrs King likes to plant and prune once in a while but mostly it's down to me.'

'Wow, it must keep you busy.'

'Busy enough,' said Henry, spooning Nescafe granules into mugs. 'But it's really just maintaining what's here now. All the hard work's been done. They've got the place just as they want so it's only about keeping on top of it all now. And I'm fortunate enough to still be pretty fit, touch wood, so it's not too much of a struggle. Not yet anyways.'

'Well, you're certainly doing a fine job. The place looks great.'

'At the moment it does but wait 'til autumn.' Henry's head shook slightly as he rattled a spoon around the mugs before offering one to Tony. 'You've never seen so many leaves. Help yourself to milk 'n sugar.'

'Thanks.' Tony got up and did just that. Two sugars and a splash of milk. 'Yes, I can imagine. Trees are ok but they do make a mess. So, Henry,' he said, lowering himself into the chair again and considering it a suitable moment to change the subject. 'What's it like here? How are the Kings to work for?'

Mrs King had seemed pleasant at the interview last week and her welcome had been warm enough on Saturday morning when Tony had moved in but he had brought his father along to help and the older man had acted as a sort of icebreaker. What Tony really wanted to know was whether she was generally that amiable or if she was just being gracious for appearances' sake. He was also keen to learn of her husband too, to know what sort of a boss he was now working for.

Henry opened the biscuit tin and pulled it to the edge of the bench. He instructed Tony to take what he wanted. He took three digestives for himself and sat down in the other chair. His glass eye stared ahead indifferently while its counterpart twinkled with amusement while appearing to seek a response to Tony's question through the glass roof.

'Well,' he began as he exhaled grandly. 'Mrs King - she's lovely. Always gracious and friendly, always happy to stop and chat. In fact, I doubt you'd find a nicer woman to work for if you tried.'

Tony could sense a 'but' looming and he didn't like it.

'Mr King though,' continued the older man. 'You haven't met him yet have you?' Tony shook his head. 'Hmm. Well, he's quite different. Not to say he's Mrs King's opposite. He's all right but you got to understand him.' He took a bite of a biscuit and continued amid the munching. 'Three things you need to remember about Mr King. One. He can be a little impatient. Two. He's a bit of a fusspot. And three… well…maybe just those two. But he does like to see initiative.'

'How do you mean?' asked Tony, reaching for a biscuit then dipping it in his coffee.

'Aw I don't know. For instance…if for some reason you ever find yourself likely to be late, let him know. Call him. They've given you a mobile, yes?' Tony nodded. Mrs King had handed him a basic handset on Saturday with all the numbers Tony was likely to need pre-programmed into it. 'Be sure to use it. He's a reasonable man and I'm sure you'll get along but he hasn't got where he is by standing out in the rain waiting for a ride.'

That actually sounded reasonable to Tony, after all, who does like standing out in the rain waiting for a ride? Though it did nothing to reduce his apprehension about picking the man up later at the airport.

Henry spoke a little more about the Kings and how he'd been quite happy working for them for close to ten years but then Tony changed the topic of conversation with a question, to which Henry's answer surprised him. The gardener, or groundskeeper as he'd probably prefer to be called, admitted that, despite having lived most of his life in the southeast, was originally from Yorkshire. Damn proud of it too. He said that work had brought his parents down in the late fifties and having settled comfortably in Maidstone, they'd never returned. However, the county, he said, was like DNA, a part of who you are.

'What about you?' Henry asked. 'You're local, I reckon.'

'Is it that obvious?'

'You don't sound like you've come far.'

'When you say it like that,' said Tony, 'my life sounds pretty unexciting doesn't it? Sometimes I wonder what it'd be like to travel around and live in other places, not just in England but around the world too.'

'Some do it. Why not you? You have any ties here?'

'Friends and family but that's about all.'

'No woman? Kids?'

'Not yet. There was a girl until a few months ago but that's history now.' Tony was relieved to no longer be with Dinah. Their constant arguing had destroyed any love he'd ever felt for her but there were undoubtedly one or two things he missed about being in a relationship.

'So nothing's keeping you really,' said Henry, in a way that seemed to get right to the bottom of the subject.

'Yeah, I don't know.' Tony wasn't convinced life was that simple.

'You're only young for a little while, friend. Don't waste it sitting around wishing for things you can just as easily go out and get.'

'That's a good philosophy to live by,' said Tony, wanting to change the subject again. 'Anyway, I never thought I might have an accent. Do I sound like a country bumpkin to you then?

'No more 'n I do to you, I expect,' replied Henry with a mouthful of biscuit.

Tony's mobile trilled in his pocket. He took it out and saw that Mrs King was calling.

'Good morning, Mrs King,' he said in his politest phone voice. He returned her pleasantries and said that yes, he was very comfortable and yes, he had found everything he needed and yes, he had met Henry. He listened a little longer and then said, 'Ok, no problem. I'll bring it round right away.' He then dropped the phone back into his pocket. 'Mrs King wants the BMW brought round. She's got to go out in a few minutes. So…' Tony drank off the rest of his coffee in one big gulp. 'Thanks for the coffee but I better get round there.'

'Righto, young fella. Anytime. See you later.'

Seven minutes later, Tony pulled the chunky X5 up outside the front of the house. He was a little unhappy with himself for not having had the foresight to wash the film of brown dirt off it but then he wasn't psychic. He wasn't to know Mrs King would want to use it and he hoped she wouldn't mind.

He took the key from the ignition and bounded up the wide-stepped porch. He pressed the small porcelain button inside the brass circle of the bell push and an urgent ring echoed behind the door. Tony refrained from peering through the glass side panels into the hallway. He didn't want to appear over-familiar. Instead, he stepped back and looked up at the grand fanlight. It was very ornate, if a tad over the top. And definitely a painter's nightmare. Its narrow veins and curved detailing would take hours to rub down and paint. He thought it looked like the top half of an elaborate steering wheel from an Old Spanish galleon, the Spanish theme continuing in the lace-like detail of the fan's outer edges.

Footsteps approached the door, which was then opened by Mrs King. She was dressed in a Laura Ashley style with daffodil coloured chinos and a pastel blue and pink flowery blouse. She looked cool and summery. She was fixing an earring as she waved Tony inside.

'You don't need to ring Tony,' she said, in an accent that was rooted somewhere in the halls of an expensive English university. 'You're part of the household now so feel free to just come on in.'

Tony was about to thank her when she continued. She seemed in a hurry. 'Simon used to leave the keys on that little table there.' She pointed to an antique half-round Queen Anne table below an unframed mirror. A crystal vase of yellow roses sat on a lace doily on its glossy surface. Simon was Tony's predecessor, the Kings' former chauffeur who had left the previous weekend having given barely any notice. He had cited a family emergency as the reason for his leaving however Mrs King suspected there was more to it. But what, she couldn't say.

Tony stepped over to the table and placed the keys on the doily.

'There's just over half a tank of petrol in it Mrs King,' he said. 'And I apologise for not having washed the car this morning for you. If I'd known you were going to want it, of course I would have done it first thing but as it was, I prepped the Bentley for later.'

'Oh don't worry about that,' she replied, stepping up to the doorway and glancing out. 'I'm not going far and certainly not anywhere special. It's not filthy is it? No, it's not. No never mind. You'll find I'm not as pernickety as my husband. What time is he coming in, by the way?'

Tony said that Mr King's plane landed at 3:15pm but admitted he hadn't checked the online schedule yet this morning to see if there were any delays. 'But I'll go and do that now,' he added.

Mrs King thanked him and walked off down the chequerboard marble floor. Tony went out and closed the door behind him.

Sitting on a stool at his breakfast bar a few minutes later, laptop open in front of him, Tony scanned the 'arrivals' page of Heathrow airport's website. It informed him that Mr King's flight from Dubai was expected to land on time into terminal 3, which gave him a little over three hours. But with this being his maiden voyage, so to speak, Tony considered it prudent to leave early.

From his recently stocked fridge, he fried up a cheese omelette. He followed that with a small pot of fruit yoghurt and then munched on an apple before slipping through to the bedroom and changing into shirt and tie. It was a stipulation that went with the job that whilst on driving duty, he must dress formally. Fortunately, the dark suit he'd had for years, the one he pulled out for funerals and job interviews still looked presentable and as he slipped on the jacket and adjusted his charcoal grey tie in the bathroom mirror, he reckoned he looked like a bona fide chauffeur. Minus the silly hat.

He glanced at his watch. It was approaching one o'clock. Right, time to hit the road.

Tony felt even more at home in the opulent interior of the Bentley with his smart togs on and he wondered if anyone seeing him drive past would think the car his. It was a silly, adolescent thought but when he glanced in the rear-view mirror, he grinned to himself and concluded that they probably would.

The Bentley's engine barely had to rouse itself as Tony threaded the big car through the lanes towards Lymbridge. The traffic in town was as heavy as usual and so rather than sticking to the main road and heading up towards the busy A21, he took a left off the high street and cut across country to wind his way towards Edenbridge with the plan to join the M25 from the A22.

It was a glorious sunny afternoon and the weather reflected Tony's mood. He truly felt blessed to be getting paid for doing such a cushy, desirable job. In fact, it didn't really feel like a job to him at all. It was quite possibly the best workday he'd had in his life so far. Above him was a cloudless expanse of blue sky. To either side and hidden behind hedgerows reverberating to all manner of insect and bird life were symmetrically aligned orchards and farmland stretching out over the undulating landscape in neatly defined four-sided shapes, like some enormous organic patchwork quilt. And in front, a unwinding ribbon of smooth, dry tarmac, for the most part empty as it wasn't a direct cut-through from any point A to B.

About twenty pleasant minutes into his journey, Tony saw two figures a little way off standing by the verge. One of them moved into the middle of the lane and began waving frantically as the Bentley approached. As he drew nearer and slowed, Tony could see there had been an accident. Twenty or so metres ahead opposite the apex of a corner, the rear underside of a car was visible above the grassy verge; its petrol tank and exhaust a dry muddy brown colour and its rear light clusters staring like dazed, bloodied eyes up at the wide blue yonder. The rest of the car was obscured, buried in the overgrown gully.

Tony stopped the Bentley and lowered his window. The man's panic-stricken face was beside him immediately. He had smears of blood on his hands and arms. His voice was frantic.

'Please, you've got to help,' he begged. 'My wife, she's having a baby. We need to get her to the hospital.' Tony glanced at the other figure by the verge. The woman, probably in her early twenties as was the man, was bent double, arms clutched around her pregnant middle as though letting go would cause it to fall to the ground. Her face was shiny and red and contorted by anguish and pain and her cheeks were damp from crying. The pale blue maternity dress she was wearing showed dark patched evidence of blood between her thighs. She also had blood on her face from a wound on her forehead.

Several things rushed into Tony's mind at that moment all with a common thread. If I help these people, how will it affect my arrival at Heathrow? It is my first day after all and the only first impression I can give my boss. I really don't want it to be anything less than my best. But no sooner had the thoughts entered his mind than they vanished again, out-voted by common decency and overpowered by the willingness to assist in the situation that he had stumbled into.

'Have you phoned for an ambulance?' he asked, removing his seatbelt and stepping out.

'My phone's got no reception here and there's no time anyway.' The man hurried over to his wife who moaned aloud and begged her husband to do something. 'It's okay Babe. We're gonna get you to the hospital. Just hold on.' He ducked his head under her arm, put his right arm around her back and very gently coaxed her towards the Bentley. Tony opened the rear door, slipped off his jacket and spread it out across the rear seat. Things were likely to get messy; the least he could do was minimise the damage to the leather interior. He then took the woman's other side and joined in with her pigeon-stepped progress towards the car. Accompanied by some very unpleasant screaming, the man helped settle his wife on the back seat then raced around to the other door. Tony got in and belted up again.

'The overnight…bag,' gasped the woman between painful breaths. 'I'll need it. It's…got everything in.' Despite her situation and her young age she was already thinking as a mother.

The young man swore and got out again. He raced across to the car wreck and disappeared into the gully.

'Which hospital do you want me to take you to?' asked Tony, nervously thinking about the time ticking away and the fact that he was about to drive away from his all-important rendezvous with his boss.

'The…new Tunbridge Wells please,' she replied through stifled excursions to contain her pain.

'Isn't that the one where the old Pembury hospital used to be?'

'Yes.'

Tony completed a three-point turn in readiness for when the man returned and after what seemed much longer than it actually was, he got back in the Bentley with a large shoulder bag clamped under his arm.

'Ok, hold tight,' said Tony, as he accelerated back down the lane the way he had just come. 'I'll try to make this as smooth as I can.'

'We need to get to the old Pembury hospital,' said the man.

'He knows.' snapped the woman. 'I've told him alre…aaarrrggghhh!!' Another wave of pain surged within her and left her sobbing.

'Please hurry,' said the man, gripping his wife's left hand as though his entire existence depended on it.

Tony knew absolutely nothing about giving birth but he'd seen it happen enough times on TV dramas to remember that a certain breathing technique could help the expectant mother. He also thought it would be useful to try to get her focus away from the pain.

'Ok, well. Hi, I'm Tony,' he began, 'and I'm glad I came along. Now, what can I call you both?'

'Matt,' said the man, too concerned for his wife and unborn child to be overly enthusiastic at introductions. 'And Joanne.'

'Good. Now Joanne, I'm no expert but isn't there some sort of breathing they say you should do?'

'I'm trying to,' she replied, weakly attempting to regulate her breathing as she'd been shown.

'That's good,' said Tony, throwing a concerned eye at his passengers in the rear-view mirror. 'So, is this your first child?'

'Yes,' said Matt. Joanne nodded too and then burst into tears. 'Come on Babe,' said Matt, stroking his wife's hair. 'Please try to hold on. Just a little longer.'

'Something's wrong with my baby,' she sobbed. 'I can feel it. It's hurting too much.' Suddenly her cries became a full-bodied wail as another round of pain gripped her. It was a dreadful, primitive sound and Tony began praying for a miraculously clear run up to the hospital doors. Very briefly, he wondered why it was that some women go through childbirth more than once if it hurt so much.

The big Bentley was far from agile in the turns and the front wheels struggled for grip if Tony carried too much speed. But with his desire to keep the ride as smooth as possible for his passengers, Tony learned to slow down before the corners and to accelerate hard out of them. Once or twice he had to use a good part of the grassy verge to pass an oncoming car but mercifully, the lane was generally clear.

At the junction with the A26, the north south route from Maidstone to Newhaven, they had to wait for several minutes when the stream of traffic seemed reluctant to let them out. This short moment of being stationary when any forward movement meant being closer to assistance was agonising for them all particularly as Joanne's screams increased in intensity every time a tsunami of pain engulfed her. Something else to increase alarmingly was Tony's feeling of helplessness and until a gap in the traffic allowed them to continue, he had an awful vision of Joanne giving birth right there on the back seat. God only knows what Mr King would have to say about that!

Twelve hair-raising minutes later, Tony swung the Bentley into the hospital's approach road and drove straight up to A&E. He pulled up behind a parked ambulance outside the sliding doors of the entrance and ran inside to get help while Matt drew his wailing wife out of the car.

Tony's appeals inside the cool, air-conditioned reception area for assistance with a pregnant woman were brief. Two nurses in pale blue uniforms who were probably already doing something important rushed towards him with questions he didn't really hear. His nerves were too frayed at that moment to do anything more than turn around and rush straight back out through the doors towards the Bentley. Fortunately, the nurses were capable of acting somewhat calmer under such circumstances and on seeing Matt struggle towards the entrance with his pregnant wife hunched against him as though she were sheltering from a storm that affected only her, they dashed forward wheelchair at the ready. Tony watched as the two nurses coaxed Joanne into the chair then sped her away through the doors and into the corridors of medical safety with Matt running alongside, concern aging his young features.

Dazed. That's how Tony felt at that moment. Like someone had placed a huge bell over his head and clobbered it a couple of times with a large hammer. To be in close confines with someone screaming at the top of their lungs for half an hour had drained his energy and impaired his hearing. That was most likely why he failed to hear the arrival of another ambulance to the A&E entrance. And it wasn't until the on-board paramedics had rushed indoors with a body on a stretcher that he realised the Bentley was blocked in. With an ambulance in front and another close up behind, Tony saw that even though his job here was done and it was now time to get the hell to Heathrow, he wasn't going anywhere until one of the ambulances moved.

He looked at his watch. Five past two. An hour and ten minutes before Mr King's plane lands. Damn. Things were beginning to look bad for his first impression. Even with a clear run, Heathrow was an hour and a quarter away and Tony knew that a clear run, even at this time of day was about as likely as him moving one of the ambulances out of the way with nothing more than the power of his mind.

He went back inside the hospital and looked for the paramedics. Maybe a simple request to back their ambulance up a bit would be all that was needed. But scanning the reception area proved fruitless. There was plenty of activity and noise but the paramedics weren't around, just staff doing staff things and several dozen people in varying states of sufferance sitting in chairs while waiting to be seen to by a nurse or doctor. Tony looked at his watch again. Only a minute had passed but it felt like more. He was getting nervous. He had to leave for the airport now or he would have to take Henry's advice and telephone Mr King to inform him that he'd been delayed. Not an enviable prospect for his first day. Having said that, he considered his excuse a valid one; i.e. he was running late on account of an unselfish act of compassion. How could Mr King think badly of him for that? He had stopped to help a pregnant woman for God's sake. Surely that was noble enough reason to be a little late. Mr King hasn't got where he is today by standing around in the rain waiting for a ride.

Tony approached the reception desk and mouthed to a slim mousy woman with a phone stuck in the crook of her neck if she knew where the ambulance drivers were. She frowned and shook her thin head at him, obviously not understanding what he had asked. She adjusted the phone's position and then began scribbling something on a large pad of paper, grunting in the affirmative ever few seconds. He then called to a nurse behind the desk who was fishing through a filing cabinet for something that she obviously couldn't find. She looked up wearily at him but ignored his call and continued searching in a lower draw, fingers walking desperately across its contents. Tony looked around hopelessly, sensing his new job and cosy little flat slipping away with each passing minute. Sweat soaked his torso and he could feel the chill of it all over his body. God, his white cotton shirt must look transparent with it by now.

He considered that he could probably move one of the ambulances himself if the keys were left in it. True, it could get him a telling off but if it'd mean he could leave now and save his job, it had to be worth it. At least he had to try. Some kind of action was needed. So he headed back out the doors into the warm afternoon sun. But as he peered into the second ambulance's driver side window a voice called out from behind.

'Excuse me Sir. Can I help you?'

He turned to see a female approaching. She was dressed in the green uniform of a paramedic. She was short and stocky but quite attractive in a Munchkin sort of way and her frown quickly changed to a smile once Tony explained himself.

'Oh thank God,' he exclaimed. 'Please. Can you move your ambulance so I can get out? I've just dropped off a very pregnant lady and I need to get going or I'll be late for my job.' His relief overshadowed any guilt he might have felt at being suspected of about to steal an ambulance.

'Sure. For a moment there I thought you were about to take something that wasn't yours.' She was carrying a plastic cup of something in one hand and reams of paperwork in the other. 'Would you mind opening the door for me?'

Tony did as she asked. She threw the paperwork on top of the already cluttered dashboard and climbed up into the driver's seat. She then rested the cup in a holder and slotted the key into the ignition.

'Nice car,' she said, indicating the Bentley with a gesture that originated from her chin. She gave the key a twist and the ambulance's diesel engine clattered into life.

'Thanks,' said Tony. 'And thanks.' He gave her a quick smile and she returned it as, leaving her door open, she backed up.

'No problem,' she called over the din of the engine.

The rear door of the Bentley was still open but before closing it, Tony grabbed his jacket from the rear seat. A large dark patch of blood was drying on the pale silk lining but at least it hadn't soaked through to the seat. Not that he could see anyway. A closer inspection would be needed when he had more time. Tony folded the jacket carefully and placed it in the Bentley's cavernous boot. He then settled himself behind the wheel and checked his watch.

It was sixteen minutes past two.

This really wasn't the kind of frantic journey he had in mind when he left home an hour and a quarter ago. But, as the world and its uncle knows, shit happens. One can only do one's best. Notwithstanding these thoughts of wisdom, Tony was understandably worried and he drove the big Bentley in anger. Controlled anger but anger nonetheless.

All the way up the A21, he was teasing the speed limit and urging anyone in his way to move over. A few cars overtook him, daring to destroy the seventy-mile an hour limit but Tony wasn't that comfortable gambling with his licence on such regularly patrolled roads. His licence was his livelihood after all. Bursts of eighty were as quick as he was willing to go. The Bentley took it all in its stride.

He made it to the M25 in fifteen minutes and merged into the flow of traffic on the UK's busiest road feeling a little more positive. He calculated that if Mr King landed on time at 3:15, he would still need to get off the plane, go through passport control and collect his luggage. This would take at least ten or fifteen minutes and possibly more and so it was likely that Tony still had an hour to arrive and to park. So providing there were no hold-ups, he stood a good chance of being on time. He hoped. He prayed.

Please God, let me make a good first impression.

It suddenly dawned on him that having not met Mr King he hadn't a clue what the man looked like. And vice versa. So unless he could find something in the car to write KING on he would have to call him and let him know where he was. Tony dismissed the thought for later and concentrated on the motorway.

Maybe it was the time of day or maybe he was just lucky but the going was good and although the motorway was busy it kept flowing. The only places where traffic backed up were at a couple of the major exits. When Tony joined the M4 it was 3:13. He prayed that there wouldn't be a queue going into the airport. He was very nearly there. Butterflies turned cartwheels in his stomach. Outside his window, planes roared overhead, their landing gear down, their tyres ready to squeal on the concrete runway. He wondered if Mr King was on any of them. He followed the arrows for terminal 3, gliding beneath bridges and flyovers at a far sedater pace than he had been travelling at several minutes ago. He pulled into a short stay car park, grabbed a ticket from the barrier and drove around the cool, dark insides of the concrete structure looking for a space. Finding one, he parked up, turned off the engine and let out a huge sigh of relief. He was wired.

It was 3:24.

He couldn't believe he'd made it in one hour and eight minutes and just how lucky he'd been with the traffic. It felt almost miraculous. He searched the glove box for something to write on but saw nothing suitable. So he got out and tucked in his still clammy shirt and straightened his tie. He then locked up the car with a blip of the fob and followed the directions for Arrivals. Once out of the car park and in the terminal, he checked his mobile phone to see if Mr King had called.

No he hadn't.

A good sign. Perhaps. With any luck he was still making his way through passport control. Tony found his way to the Arrivals concourse and found a space aside from the crowds of others waiting. Then his mobile trilled.

It was Mr King.

More short stories by M.K. Aston

Once Upon a Somewhere